BREAK THROUGH

BREAK THROUGH

Terri Cutshall

WRITEWAY PUBLISHING
Raleigh, North Carolina
www.writewaypublishing.com

Breakthrough

Printed in the United States of America
First Printing 2020

ISBN 978-1-946425-63-8 print

Book Design by CSinclaire Write-Design
Cover Design by Klevur

WRITEWAY PUBLISHING

Raleigh, North Carolina
www.writewaypublishing.com

This book is dedicated to my wife
Melissa
and to my amazing family and friends.
Thank you for believing in me even when I don't.
You keep me grounded; you keep me moving forward;
and most importantly, you keep me laughing.

For Heather
I will always treasure
the unbreakable bond we share.

For Mom
You are my lighthouse.

You are loved.

CONTENTS

ACKNOWLEDGMENTS

I am especially grateful to Marcey Rader, Productivity Consultant, Speaker, and Author for expressing upon me her opinion that "you can't write a book and not publish it."

A sincere thank you to my dream team—Bobbi Diehl, Cheryl Alles, Dawn MacGibbon, Hannah Braundel, Heather Henry, Kathleen Kuschel, Katie Henry, Kelly Daughtry, Lisa Brewer, Lisa Theet, Lisa Thompson, Mandy Perryman, Melissa Kuschel, Sandra Thompson, Sally Soika, and Tammy Cutshall—for your interest, feedback, support, and words of encouragement throughout this process. I truly appreciate all of you. Thank YOU.

Special thanks to my editor, Lee Heinrich and Write Way Publishing for agreeing to take on an extreme novice who had a story to tell. Thank you, Lee. Your guidance and gentle nudges in the right direction turned what I once viewed as disappointing, failed attempts into eagerly anticipating iterations while learning the craft. As goal oriented as I'm wired, I may never reach storytelling master status, but in this case, the journey has been worth the wait. And I don't want this journey to come to an end. I thank you for that.

CHAPTER
One

Friday

"When was the last time you got laid?" Rachel asked as she gave Madison a toothy grin and yanked an olive from her martini's swizzle stick.

"Rachel!" Madison gasped.

"Well?"

"It's been awhile," Madison hissed at her ex-girlfriend.

"Then if you're not taking *me* home with you, you need to pick another hottie in here and take her home. You need to work off that bitchy edge, Miss Madison Thornton."

"Wow, I had forgotten how much of a phallus you could be."

"Oh god, Madison. You can say the word dick you know. It won't kill you."

Madison responded with a sigh and a roll of her eyes.

"You know I love you, babe," Rachel teased and

wrinkled her nose. She scanned the room, her eyes quickly floated across the dance floor area, not yet in full swing, and landed on a brunette with shoulder-length hair. She was leaning against the bar, talking to one of the bartenders. The woman smiled at something the bartender said.

"Over there. Her," Rachel said.

"I can't."

"Okay, so no one-night stand. Just do some flirting and see where it goes. It will do you some good. Seriously. Got to pee." Rachel stood and walked away before Madison could protest.

Shit. Shit. Shit. "Here goes nothing," she mumbled. She gulped down the last of her cocktail and pushed herself from the booth, knowing that if Rachel came out of the bathroom and she was still sitting in their booth, Rachel would walk right up to the pretty woman and say something to embarrass the hell out of her.

Madison walked up to the bar and stopped beside the woman, leaving a comfortable distance between them, and motioned for the bartender. She casually looked over at the woman's drink and asked, "What are you drinking?"

From this proximity it was easy to take in the fine details of the stranger's face. Her silky complexion had no more than a light layer of makeup. Except for her eyes. They were enveloped by onyx eye liner and mascara that thickened her eyelashes, which Madison ventured to guess were naturally long all on their own. Her slight smile pulled Madison's gaze to rest on her full lips, glossy and dark maroon.

"I'm sorry?" the woman asked.

"What are you drinking, and does it have enough alcohol in it?" Madison asked. The other woman's expression was one of confusion.

"You know how some bars skimp on the alcohol and charge an arm and a leg for a glass of juice." Madison watched as acknowledgment washed over the woman's face and her expression softened. *Beautiful smile*, Madison thought.

"Yes, it's got a kick to it. This is an amaretto sour."

"Good. That's what I want to hear," Madison said and momentarily locked eyes with the woman. She reluctantly pulled her eyes away. "I'll have what she's having."

She felt the other woman's eyes on her while she busied herself by withdrawing her credit card from the pocket on her phone case. With drink in hand, she leaned toward the woman and whispered, "If you get bored with the friends you're here with, come dance with me later. I'll be over there," she motioned to the far corner with her free hand and added, "with my friend." Madison gave the woman a quick side glance along with a smile that revealed her dimples and walked away.

Rachel was already re-seated in the booth and trying not to stare at what was happening at the bar. She started her verbal assault even before Madison sat back down.

"Well? What happened?"

Hoping to appease her but doubting it would,

Madison replied, "I flirted with her."

"And?"

"*And* if she's interested, I asked her to come dance with me later."

"*Is* she interested?"

"I don't know, Rachel. She hasn't come over here yet." Madison used her boss tone that Rachel despised.

"Well, did you do it right?" Rachel asked, headed down the well-worn path to argument central, when as partners, she was inclined to stop off and change course. Relieved that those days were in the distant past, Madison just glared at her.

"Are you seriously asking me if I flirted with her correctly? You are incorrigible!"

The dance floor filled quickly. Dancing was something Madison and Rachel had been able to do well together. They were laughing and having a good time moving to the fast-paced, throw-back college tunes when Madison felt something nudge her in the back. When she turned around the woman from the bar was standing in front of her. She stood a couple inches taller now that she wasn't leaning against the bar. Madison had missed that detail earlier.

The brunette leaned in closer to be heard over the music. "I'm sorry. I didn't mean to bump into you."

Madison shrugged and said, "No problem. I'm Madison."

"Brooke," the woman replied.

They enjoyed dancing together to a couple songs before Madison realized Rachel must have slipped off somewhere to leave the two of them alone. Madison stilled as Brooke suddenly leaned in and spoke into her ear.

"I'm going to grab another drink. Do you need one?"

Madison's ear blushed as Brooke's lips made contact, and her warm breath sent a shiver down her spine. Madison managed a nod, and in an instant, the woman was gone. When she returned with a drink in each hand, Brooke motioned for Madison to follow her. She guided them away from the loud music.

Bottoms up and the tall woman leaned in to tease Madison's ear again, this time lightly touching Madison's forearm as well. A tingle spread on Madison's bare skin and marched, as if on a quest, to meet up with the shiver traveling down her spine. *Holy hormones*, Madison thought.

"Where did you learn to dance so well?" Brooke asked.

Madison's cheeks flushed as she became conscious of her body's reaction. "A lot of college parties," she said with a laugh, "and for me, dancing is a good stress reliever, so I get a lot of practice."

"I can think of other ways to blow off steam," Brooke said seductively, her dark brown eyes deepening to black. Madison felt her pulse quicken at the proposition and momentarily felt inclined to flirt back and follow Rachel's advice. That is until she reminded herself of how truly terrible she was at one-night stands. The exactly two times she had engaged in said activity ended in utter disappointment because she couldn't keep her need for emotional attachment in check, ergo, out of it. Her supposed one-night stands turned into weeks of emotional recovery. Not worth it.

"Oh, I'm sure you can," Madison said, allowing her eyes to wander up and down Brooke's very capable body, her libido very much wishing she would respond differently, "but dancing works the best for me." A look of something Madison perceived as confusion, maybe disappointment, flashed across the woman's countenance.

"Well then at least save me a dance the next time, okay?" The woman raised an eyebrow, flashed what could only be called a you-are-going-to-regret-this-in-the-morning smile, and walked away before waiting for a response. Even after the rejection, the confidence in her demeanor never wavered.

The woman must not get turned down often. Madison watched her leave, feeling an ache in her gut that was definitely not going to be quenched by dance music.

Monday

Alex Bennett stood in her lab reviewing the latest test results with Patricia when Trevor called. Trevor was Alex's coordinator, and he was extremely good at keeping Alex on schedule. Trevor was about ten years younger than Alex, responsible, and loved his job. He was good-looking and dressed impeccably metro. Alex had offered him his first professional job. He actively exhibited his gratefulness on a daily basis, appreciative for her mentorship.

"Alex, your sister just called to let you know that the Pharmacist Consultant you requested will be here at one o'clock. Do you want to use the conference room or your office?"

"My office, please. Thank you, Trevor." Alex smiled, glad that her sister had come through for her so quickly. She returned her attention to Patricia and their conversation.

"We have almost all the data entered into the new system. By our next meeting I should be able to show you the molecular rendering through the use of our new 3D hologram application," Patricia said, moving through multiple screens with ease. Alex's senior by close to twenty years, Patricia had spent most of her career in research and development. As the lead lab technician, her many years of experience were invaluable to Alex's team.

Happy with her team's progress, Alex recognized Patricia's efforts and said, "I'm looking forward to seeing the binding step via this virtual 3D technology. Thank you, everyone." Today was shaping up to be a good day.

At twelve forty-five, Trevor looked up to see an attractive woman walking up to his desk. "Hi. I'm Madison Thornton. I'm here to see Miss Bennett."

Madison followed Trevor through a glass door adorned with a shiny metal plate bearing the name Alexandria Bennett. He offered her a seat in front of a large desk. The floor to ceiling windows in the room afforded a beautiful view of the city. When her gaze returned to survey the room, she immediately noticed how organized the items on the desk were. In fact, as her eyes moved over the rest of the room, she noticed that everything in the room was neat and orderly.

She didn't know a lot about Alex, only that she was Amber's younger sister by about four years. She had seen a picture of the two of them from Alex's college graduation on Amber's desk. *That picture must be over ten years old by now*, she thought. Being closer to Amber's age herself, Madison figured that put Alex in her mid-thirties. She recalled the sweet and eager look on the girl's face in the photo with her beautiful smile and twinkle in her eyes, as if she were ready to set off from college and change the world.

Amber had called her two weeks ago asking if she would be interested in consulting with Alex on her genetics project. Amber would have done it herself, but she was head of the general continuing education programs for the American Pharmaceutical Association, whereas Madison was in charge of the specialty programs, and genetics was a closer fit to her areas of expertise. Madison had only a moment's hesitation about accepting due to her heavy workload demands, because these unique consulting opportunities always fueled her fire. There was never a limit to learning in the field of science. And besides, she didn't have to bake in commute time since their buildings were within walking distance of each other. The beautifully architected Biogenetics Lab was adjacent to her APhA building, located on the only privately-owned space within the surrounding areas of the National Mall in Washington, D.C.

Trevor gestured that Miss Thornton was waiting in Alex's office. *Excellent*, Alex thought. *She's prompt.* Structure, discipline, and being on time made her happy. Through her office door she saw the back of the woman with long blond hair pulled back in a tasteful hair tie. She was seated in front of Alex's desk.

"Miss Thornton. Good afternoon. How are you?" Alex absently extended her hand in greeting as the woman stood.

"Miss Bennett. It's nice to meet you."

Their hands and eyes connected. They both froze.

Alex was immediately overwhelmed by the woman's alluring perfume, slightly familiar, and her striking tailored pants suit that molded perfectly to her body. Matching heels set her eye level with Alex. Her eyes immediately roamed over the same body that she had watched dance, incredibly well as she recalled, only days before. When her eyes finally migrated back up to find deep blue eyes, her mind momentarily went blank. This stranger was even more beautiful in the bright light of day. *How is the woman from the bar standing here in my office? Holy shit.* She pumped her hand up and down one more time as she spoke.

"I'm staring, I'm sorry." *How rude.* "How is it that you are *here*?"

"Amber asked me," Madison said without breaking eye contact.

"*You're* the consultant?" Alex asked in disbelief.

Madison nodded.

"And Friday, was what, a coincidence? You didn't know who I was?" Alex asked. Each word came out of her mouth slowly and fully enunciated as if she was addressing someone not familiar with the English language.

"No, I didn't." Madison's face radiated sincerity. Alex believed her.

Alex forced herself to pull her eyes away and walked around the desk to take a seat. Alex cleared her throat and spoke first, "Please, call me Alex."

"Alex?" Madison hesitated, "I thought your name was Brooke." The slight grin that formed on her face did not go unnoticed.

"Well, this is embarrassing," Alex dropped her head and seemed to concentrate on a fascinating speck of dust on her desk. "I use my middle name at the bar with strangers." *Strangers that have a strong potential to become one-night stands, that is.*

"Well then," Madison smiled, "it's nice to meet you, *Alex*, and I'm doing well, thanks for asking."

Alex regained her composure and pulled her attention back to the task at hand. "What has Amber shared with you?" The two women fell into their professional personas with ease.

"Full transparency, not much, only that you are looking for a consultant on your genetics project." Madison fell silent and waited for Alex to take the lead.

"I'm at a point in my research where I need you." Alex's lower than usual tone made her pause. She cleared her throat to make an adjustment and continued. "I need access to more expertise in the fields of pharmacokinetics and pharmacodynamics. We are studying Tamoxifen's drug action on the breast cancer gene mutation, or the BRCA gene, and I need to understand in more depth the drug absorption and metabolic pathways that affect individual responses to drugs, both regarding therapeutic effect as well as adverse events. My sister tells me your department is responsible for specialized pharmacy areas. I assume that includes genetics?"

"Yes," Madison answered. "Genetics is an area under my team's purview as well as a personal interest of mine."

"Then you are familiar with pharmacogenetic testing and personalized medicine," Alex stated more than asked, and Madison nodded. Alex continued, "Last year we spent a lot of time studying individual genotypes for genes that encode for drug metabolizing enzymes. We leveraged the research output from the Biobank, the largest "Big Data" human sequencing resource effort to date. It was a Life Sciences Industry Consortium that brought together the thought to link human genetic variations to human biology and disease. As you can imagine, since one gene is inherited from each parent there were a lot of combinations to test. We now have created a database for those combinations of genes and their unique instructions for making enzymes." Alex's face was animated and her eyes sparkled as she spoke.

Madison continued to sit quietly, eyes intent on Alex.

Alex received Madison's gaze to mean she was still very interested in the level of knowledge she was sharing.

"As you know, many drugs require enzymes for activation, metabolism, or both, and drug metabolizing enzymes are commonly influenced by genetic variations. We are now at a point in our study where we need to solve for a way to stunt the enzyme activity from breaking down the Tamoxifen hybrid molecule too quickly, since we need it to stay attached to the BRCA gene mutation in order to silence it or block it from causing future harm. This is where I would need you to focus your attention. How does that sound to you?" Alex watched Madison's reaction.

Madison was introspective for only a moment before responding, "Alex, a primary function of my team is to create continuing education for pharmacists, so we put together informational segments on topics for one or two credits at a time. An example would be the use of genetic material to manipulate our body's cells to treat an inherited or acquired disease. But I've never actually seen it happen." Madison hoped Alex would offer to show her the lab at some point. "Understanding and studying the part metabolizing enzymes play is part of the learning series, so I at least have a really good place to start."

Pleased with the way the conversation was progressing, Alex continued, "Another important factor is the fact that genetic material inserted directly into cells is typically not functional, so we leverage genetically engineered vectors to deliver the healthy genes into the cells. The most effective vector to date is a modified form of a virus. We study how to alter the virus so that it will be able to enter the cell, but it will not be capable of infecting the cell or the human host."

Her interest piqued, Madison quickly interjected, "And once the modified virus enters the cell, it integrates the healthy genetic material it's carrying right into the chromosomes, and for some unknown reason, this integration acts as a catalyst for the host's immune system and triggers an immediate attack on the mutated portion of the chromosome, leaving only healthy genes behind."

A small smile tugged at the corner of Alex's mouth as she said, "That's right. I am impressed."

Madison was already thinking about how she could provide the most helpful assistance as she processed the conversation and watched Alex quietly. Alex's phone chirped. It was a message from Trevor reminding her of her next meeting. Alex put her phone down and picked up the conversation where she had left off. Madison entertained her own thoughts as her mind flooded with scenarios and possibilities playing out in her head.

"So, what do you think? Are you interested in being my partner on this?" Enthusiasm emanated from Alex as she spoke.

Madison was snapped back to the present when she heard the word partner, the use of the word insinuating a much different meaning. It prompted her to take another moment before she responded. It was difficult to resist Alex's energy, both verbal and nonverbal. It was like invisible gravity rings that spread out and enveloped everything around her, exerting a pull toward her as she reached each new level of excitement.

"What do I think?" Madison repeated. Alex nodded

with a raised eyebrow that caused an unexpected flutter low in Madison's belly. Even here in the office, that eyebrow play seemed seductive. "I think you may have a hard time getting rid of me."

"Then it's settled."

They finished their discussion by deciding that Monday and Wednesday afternoons would best suit Madison to be physically in the lab. Tuesdays and Thursdays were way too crazy for her and Fridays were devoted to meetings and conference calls with the rest of the pharmacy faculty.

Madison walked the short distance back across the street to her office in a daze. She felt her excitement build as she thought about the project. Learning something new and being able to provide her expertise at the same time never got old for her, but after being in her field for ten plus years, the newness had worn off a long time ago. This particular project felt different. Maybe it was the personal pull to the science itself that sparked her interest or maybe it was Alex's enthusiasm in presenting her case and her animation as she described her work with such passion.

Whatever it was, it was fun to watch. Brooke, no Alex, was fun to watch. She realized that Alex was more than that sweet girl in the photo on Amber's desk. She was a confident, competent, witty woman who had been able to connect with her intellectually. How could this be the same woman she was extremely physically attracted to as well? *Wow*, she thought. Few people were able to surprise her but here, within two unexpected meetings, this woman was able to thoroughly intrigue her.

Anticipation coursed through her body. She replayed their initial interactions over again in her mind, beginning with their dancing and then with their handshake. Had Alex really fumbled her words and held on to her hand a bit too long? And the almost huskiness in her voice when she said she needed her. *Had that really happened?* She shook the thought away. "It's just been too long since you've had an attractive woman look at and talk to you that way," she muttered. She wasn't short on other women finding her attractive, but to be able to spar with one intellectually was impressive. Besides, she had no idea what Alex's intentions were or if she would have an interest in her. Especially if she would have accepted an invitation to a one-night stand.

Either way, it was a moot point now that they were going to be working together. And it would be extremely unprofessional to make it anything more than that. She did enjoy the emotional lift it gave her though, from the flirting the other night to seeing those dark eyes look at her in that way today. She decided to ride out the high for as long as it lasted.

Alex stopped at the bar after work, her usual routine one or two nights a week. Callie Mason, Alex's best friend since their undergraduate days, winked at her from behind the counter. "What's it going to be today, red or white?"

"Hmm, I think today's a red kind of day. I want an order of wings too. Please," she added with a grin.

"Grab our booth. I'll join you there."

Being polar opposites, it amazed Alex that she and Callie had ever became friends. In college, Alex had her head in a book, always reading or studying. Callie was a social butterfly with a photographic memory. She rarely attended classes because of her amazing mental recall. On top of that, she had a trust fund that allowed her the flexibility to drop out of graduate school and travel the world. Differences aside, something clicked early on between them. After trying out the dating thing, they mutually decided that their bond was driven more by friendship, one they had cherished ever since. By the time Alex graduated, she had two small totes filled with the postcards and tchotchkes Callie had sent her from all the exciting places she had visited. When Callie's traveling had run its course, she opened a bar to continue her social networking from a stationary location.

"Here you go, gorgeous," Callie said, as she took a seat across from Alex. "How was your day?"

"Interesting." Alex paused, deciding where to begin.

Callie leaned in. She beamed with pride as she thought about how determined and courageous her best friend was. She knew how hard Alex had worked to graduate magna cum laude with a Ph.D. in Genetics. Just four years ago, at age thirty-one, she had been offered the prestigious role of Research Director at Biogenetics. Callie was in awe of Alex's stamina and dedication to her work focused on Pharmacogenomics and the incredible responsibility for fulfilling the requirements of the grant money she had recently secured. Callie felt it was her responsibility to help Alex maintain a work-life balance. Callie took her role very seriously knowing that Alex's research had a way of totally consuming her if she wasn't careful, forcing everything else and everyone to take a back seat.

"I met Madison Thornton today."

"Who's that?"

"Amber referred her to me as a Pharmacist Consultant. She's not at all what I expected. I assumed Amber would send a graduate student or a recent graduate knee deep in research, but that is not at all who showed up." Alex fell silent.

"You should see the look on your face right now. She must have really made an impression on you."

"That's because she's the same woman from the bar Friday night."

"What do you mean?"

"You remember the woman I was dancing with?"

"The hot blond, yeah. Hard to forget," Callie said as she straightened to attention.

"Yeah, well that's who Amber sent to my office today."

"No shit!" Callie exclaimed. Alex chuckled. She enjoyed it when Callie gobbled up her stories like a woman dieting on a free calorie day.

"Today she had her hair pulled off her face and with the heels she was wearing, she stood about my height." She paused and then added, "Callie, I wish you could have seen her. She was wearing a Ralph Lauren pants suit that showed off her curves so well I forgot what to say after I introduced myself, and I started stammering. She had this air of confidence and sophistication about her but not in a snobby sort of way. She easily kept up with the conversation and, I would only admit this to you, I was somewhat intimidated by her."

"What? Could you have finally met your match?" Callie teased.

"I don't know *that* much about her yet. Let's not get ahead of ourselves. And besides, you know I suck at relationships."

"Who said anything about a relationship? You just need to put yourself out there again."

"I'm doing that now with Michael," Alex said with a sly grin. She was referring to the occasional evenings spent blowing off steam with her hot co-worker.

"I don't mean sex, and you know it. I mean putting yourself out there when it involves a risk of really feeling something."

"Yeah, and we both know how well that ended up last time, don't we?"

"I'm not talking about Kate either, Alex. No one can take anything from you until you give something first. Alex, look at me. We are getting a little ahead of ourselves again, aren't we?"

Alex nodded. "Of course I am, because that's what I do," Alex conceded.

Callie immediately started scheming. "Ok, so first, we need to find out more about this Madison."

Alex laughed at the enthusiasm in Callie's voice. "You love this, don't you?"

"Ah, yeah, sure I do!"

Alex laughed again, but her chest tightened.

Wednesday

Two days later, Alex and Madison were huddled in the conference room. Alex knew that the pharmacist in Madison understood safety and efficacy development through phased clinical trials more so than discovery, the initial step in the research process. She focused the discussion with Madison on the pre-clinical work involved.

Alex picked up her pen and began twirling it between her fingers. "Today's healthcare model supports placing a woman diagnosed with breast cancer on a regimen of Tamoxifen therapy. Once inside the body, metabolizing enzymes break down the Tamoxifen molecule into active metabolites that fight the cancer cells." Alex paused and looked pensive.

"The fact is that gene mutations predispose individuals to cancer because that's where the integrity of our DNA is compromised. Cancer is smart. It capitalizes on the weak links in our DNA. I don't think we'd be doing our due diligence if we didn't focus our research more upstream. Instead of focusing on a way to beat down the cancer cells after they have already attacked the mutation, we home in on the gene mutation itself and search for ways to ward off the cancer cells from ever attacking it to begin with.

"My team is developing that safety cap, so to speak,

that once introduced into the body, will seek, find, and shield the mutated site. Starting with existing molecular entities that are used to treat the disease, we tweak different molecular structures searching for the right combination that will, in theory, prevent cancer cells from ever latching onto those weak links."

Madison remained silent, processing the information.

"Would it help to see the lab now?"

"Yes, it would." Madison was pleased that Alex offered and that she didn't have to ask.

Alex continued as they walked, "Madison, my research has the potential to create personalized preventive medicine for individuals whose genetic testing shows them to be predisposed to breast cancer. Prevention is a step well ahead of the need for diagnosis and treatment. Alex placed her palm on the biometrics scanner. When the door opened, she stepped aside for Madison to enter ahead of her.

Stopping just inside the room and without interrupting anyone, Alex began, "Do you recall biology lab in college when you grew colonies of bacteria in Petri dishes? Or when the class would pipette cells into small glass tubes and place them in different machines to isolate the mitochondria and DNA from the nucleus? A very popular test was isolating the gene that glows and changing it from blue to green since green in fluorescence imaging shows up more readily in scans than blue."

"Vaguely, it was so long ago," Madison answered.

"Well, some of the techniques we use here start from those fundamentals. We have three primary stations in this lab and three technicians per station." Madison noticed people congregated in groups around several different stations.

Alex pointed them out as she described each one. "The first station, over there, is the Isolation Station. Now that we know where to find the BRCA mutated gene in our DNA, Tammy's team, Chris and Lexy, extract the BRCA mutated gene and grow it or replicate it in a Petri dish in order to study it and prep it for the Binding Station."

Alex pointed again, "Over here is the Stability Station. Justin's team, Tim and Jen, take the current medication for breast cancer, Tamoxifen, and test organic molecules that bind to it permanently to form modified molecular hybrids, or MMH. We know Tamoxifen binds to gene receptors to block ill effects, but we need a molecule not only to block but to slow it down and blunt the ill effects.

"Finally, this is the Binding Station. Patricia's team, Melissa and Collin, attach the MMH from the Stability Station to the BRCA mutated gene from the Isolation Station to form a new, modified molecular gene we call BRCA-MMG. Essentially, we change the BRCA mutated gene's DNA from harmful to harmless."

Alex's enthusiasm heighted. "This essentially means that a woman could carry and live with the new, modified, molecular gene, BRCA-MMG, and experience no harmful side effects. What is even more important is that women of childbearing age would be able to pass the BRCA-MMG onto their offspring with no ill effects. No more breast cancer."

Madison looked around the room and when her gaze returned to Alex, she said, "This is absolutely incredible."

"Thank you, Madison." Her smile reached her eyes. "Let me introduce you to the team."

Alex watched Madison intently as she interacted with members of her team, asking them questions and clarifying responses. She liked Madison's easy banter and the natural way she made those around her feel comfortable. After just a brief afternoon, it felt as if she had worked alongside them for much longer than one day.

Back in the conference room, Madison reflected on the afternoon.

"Thank you for showing me around. I have so much to learn, and I have so many questions."

As Madison collected her thoughts, a crease formed between her eyebrows. Alex wanted to reach out and touch her face to smooth away the line with her thumb. The thought startled her.

"Give me your number." Alex's voice was louder than she intended as she pulled her phone from the pocket of her lab coat.

Her thoughts interrupted, Madison responded, "I'm sorry?"

"Give me your number. Feel free to call me or text me your questions as you think of them."

Alex keyed Madison's number into her phone and said, "This is me texting you now, so you have my number."

Madison tried to protest. "I know how busy you are, Alex. You brought me in to provide support for your project, not add a burden to it."

"You are not a burden, Madison." Alex's intense gaze sent a tingle down Madison's spine. Alex broke their gaze first and walked back to her seat at the table.

Trevor called a short time later to let Alex know that her meeting with Michael was in ten minutes. At the top of the hour, there was a light knock at the door, and Michael poked his head in and asked, "You ready for me, Alex?"

"Hi. Come in. Michael, this is Madison Thornton. She is the Pharmacist Consultant I mentioned yesterday."

Michael extended his hand and said, "It's a pleasure to meet you, Madison, and welcome."

"Madison, this is Michael Francis. As our head of compliance and security, he's responsible for protecting our project from any inside or outside conflicts of interest and assessing any threats. His primary role is to keep us within our compliance guardrails in order to maintain our grant status. More importantly, he protects us and our assets."

"What do you need protection from?" Madison asked, with a hint of concern.

Alex brushed the comment aside. "Nothing for you to worry about. Michael takes care of all that so we can do the fun stuff." Alex looked at Michael, and he nodded in agreement and smiled back at her. Madison noticed there was something intimate in the way Michael looked at Alex.

"How long have you worked together?" Madison asked.

"We've worked together for, what Michael, two

years now?" An unexpected stab of displeasure pierced Madison and some of the high she'd been riding on sent her descending a couple thousand feet.

Chapter Two

Wednesday

The following two weeks passed swiftly. Alex enjoyed working side by side with Madison and her interest in Madison heightened with each new conversation. She craved to know more about her personally, but that interest took a back seat to wanting Madison to have a high professional opinion of her, so anytime the conversation veered off into the personal, Alex would consciously redirect it.

Wednesday afternoon Madison arrived at Alex's office on time as always. Alex was on the phone with Patricia. She smiled when Madison came in and jumped out of her seat. "Patricia wants to see us and she's happy." Alex bounced both eyebrows up and down a couple times. "That's a good sign."

Alex led them to the entrance of a small room adjacent to the lab. When they entered the room, Madison was surprised when she didn't see microscopes and lab equipment scattered all over the place. There was an oval glass top table occupying a large portion of the room. Black leather ergonomic office chairs occupied by Patricia's team surrounded it. Madison and Alex took seats beside each other, and the technicians turned their attention to Alex. With a couple of taps from Patricia's fingers, Madison saw a 3D hologram of a molecule take shape, suspended in mid-air, above the table.

Patricia started talking first. "We are close, Alex. We may have found the first modified molecular hybrid, or MMH, that will bind to the mutated breast cancer gene." She moved the image around to illustrate. With a few keystrokes on a seemingly imaginary keyboard embedded in the tabletop, Patricia was able to manipulate the image in any way she liked.

"Is it really working?" Alex asked.

"Yes, it is really working!" Patricia exclaimed with the rest of her team chiming in to echo her excitement. Patricia's stoic nature was painfully consistent so when she broke from that mold, people noticed.

Alex asked to see the binding step again. She felt her own enthusiasm build. Patricia typed onto the tabletop keyboard, and the 3D representation of the MMH and DNA strand took shape in the space above the table. Alex took a moment to draw in a deep breath to calm her nerves before she allowed herself to bring the view into focus. Then she saw it. With video replay set on slow motion, the modified molecular hybrid attached itself to a portion of the mutated gene sequence.

Madison sat mesmerized by the sight. Her thoughts were interrupted when she heard Alex say her name. "Madison, you can see the mutated BRCA gene here." Alex pointed into dead space. "And here," pointing to another area in the air, "here is the molecule." Madison could see that the two entities were indeed connected.

"This is fascinating." Madison reached out and lightly squeezed Alex's forearm. Alex immediately felt the sensation of Madison's warm touch travel the length of her arm. Their eyes met, and Alex reveled in this moment shared between them.

"It sure will be when we can get that molecule to bind to that gene and stay there long enough to do its job." Alex returned her gaze to the image suspended in perpetual motion.

The team used the remainder of the afternoon to discuss next steps for the time studies to understand how long the binding would need to last to be effective enough to alter the gene's susceptibility to infection and disease. When they had gathered enough information to keep moving forward, Alex suggested a team dinner for Friday.

"This is cause for celebration," Alex said, as she looked around the table at everyone's exhausted but exhilarated expressions. She asked Patricia to get a final head count by Friday morning so Trevor could call and make a reservation. Madison walked with Alex back to her office to collect her things before leaving.

Taking advantage of the privacy the space offered Alex said, "You are welcome to join us at dinner Friday.

You know, since you are part of the team now."

Madison smiled and thanked Alex. "I appreciate the invite, but I'm afraid I can't. I have plans that I can't change." She thought she saw a flash of disappointment on Alex's face and immediately added, "Next time?"

"Of course. Have a good weekend, Madison."

In that moment, Alex was thankful she was quick on her feet. Their conversation around dinner had felt more like asking Madison on a date rather than inviting her to join her team celebration. And why did her decline of the offer feel more like rejection?

Alex watched Madison leave, and Trevor caught her staring down the hall when he entered the space Madison had just vacated. He pulled Alex back to the present to tell her that David wanted to see her. David was her boss. He was entitled and arrogant but very smart. Alex made her way to the elevators and rode to the top floor. *Demanding. There's one word for you*, she thought. He insisted on having the entire top floor of the building for himself and his corporate staff. He was old school, loved to use the term subordinate, and he was most agreeable with people who did what they were told without argument or questions, especially women.

Feeling annoyed but still energized from her morning meetings, she walked into David's office.

"So? Where are you with the MMH? The grant is about to expire, and the only way it will be renewed is if you have something good to tell them." Boy did he know how to pop the feel-good balloon.

Fueled by the look on the faces of her team from just

moments before, Alex ignored David's abruptness. She said, "We see MMH interested in the gene and initially binding. It's encouraging."

She did not notice Michael standing in the far corner of the room until he asked, "Does that mean success?" His smile warmed as he looked at Alex.

"MMH needs to bind to the BRCA gene long enough to protect it from being influenced by any threat of cancer, so it's not a success yet. The time studies are the next step."

"When will you have definitive proof that it works?" David asked.

"Give me a couple weeks to test its stability," Alex said.

"Get to work then. Break's over." David barked the dismissal.

Alex left David's office refusing to let go of the good feeling prompted by Patricia's news. She realized she was looking forward to dinner on Friday.

Friday

Alex's team was in high spirits at dinner Friday evening. The fact that Madison wasn't able to join them nagged at Alex, but she pushed the thought away to focus on enjoying the relaxed time with her team. The best way to describe Alex's team was dedicated and committed. They would work themselves relentlessly until they achieved the results they were looking for. This time had been no exception, and Alex could see the toll the past few weeks and months had taken on each of them.

As the evening wound down, Alex looked around the table and said, "Go home and get some well-deserved rest. Your hard work is paying off. I appreciate all of you."

Alex walked toward the exit and was surprised to see Michael approaching her.

"Did I miss the party?" He grinned and fell into step with Alex.

"I am afraid so. How did you know where we were?"

"It wasn't hard to find you with all the buzz at work today. Your team was excited to spend time with you outside of the office."

"I was looking forward to it as much as they were. We had a good time."

"Come have a drink with me. There's a bar around the corner." *Yes, there is*, she thought. *Callie's bar, in fact.*

"I really shouldn't. I've already had too much wine."

"Just one? Please? I want to celebrate with you too." Michael moved closer to Alex hoping his physical presence would help her decide. She noticed that he had changed clothes since work and now had on a nice pair of fitted jeans with a button-down shirt and a light dinner jacket. She accepted his offer, but if she was being totally honest with herself, she accepted because she was hoping to get lucky enough to run into Madison there again.

Callie waved Alex to a couple of open seats at the bar. She looked Michael up and down.

"Are we celebrating or commiserating?"

"Celebrating," Michael answered.

Callie poured two shots and directed her question to Alex, "So, no threatening letters lately?"

"Not since the last phase when the gene testing wrapped up, but David will be getting ready for the next press release soon since our grant is ready to expire, so fingers crossed nothing serious."

Callie poured herself a shot and raised her glass, "To nothing serious." Alex and Michael repeated the toast and drank. Callie left Alex and Michael to talk and returned to her other customers. She kept tabs on Alex by looking over at her every now and then. At one point she noticed Alex looking around the room. Callie knew right away who she was looking for. The next time Alex's gaze reached hers, she shook her head to answer her question.

Alex was surprisingly shaken by the disappointment raised by that single gesture from Callie. She had to consciously bring her attention back to Michael and their conversation. Her brain kept running away with her, back to that Friday night. She had played it cool when Madison had approached her at the bar, her confidence heightened by the fact that Callie was standing there with her, watching the whole thing. Not to mention the fact that seeing such a gorgeous woman appear nervous, almost unsure of herself, added another layer of excitement to the interaction. She had watched the way her long blond hair had fallen over her shoulders when she bent her head to fiddle with her credit card.

Anxious for their *tête-à-tête* to continue, Alex was

thrilled when the woman invited her to dance. Callie had made her wait to join her on the dance floor, telling her not to appear too eager. Alex had kept her seat at the bar and watched the woman dance. And boy could she dance. Madison's body moved to the music as if it were massaging every verse. Alex had so wished she could be her next piece of music. She knew she would have, without question, gone home with her, if only she had asked. But she hadn't asked.

Michael interrupted her thoughts again. "I should take you home now," Michael whispered in her ear, "to my place." They had hooked up a few times over the last couple years but had mutually agreed not to make a routine out if it. Michael usually sought her out after a break-up so she could only assume that was what generated this invitation. Welcoming the physical closeness, she started toward the exit with Michael. She needed to work off this sexual tension from wanting someone she couldn't have anyway. Win, win all around. Callie waved goodbye from behind the counter, and Alex blew her a kiss.

Half past midnight that same evening, Callie glanced at the door as four off-duty police officers in their street clothes entered the bar. They paused right inside the door to peruse the bar area. Finding it occupied, they made their way to an empty booth toward the back. It wasn't strange to see cops in this late. With multiple precincts covering the D.C. area, officers frequently stopped in to unwind after their shifts. Callie prided herself for seldomly needing to call the police to break up any disorderly conduct thanks to her bouncer, Todd Calloway. He helped her bartend, and he kept an eye on the customers.

The female officer in the group moved to the bar. After getting Callie's attention, she ordered four draft beers. Callie felt the dark-haired woman watching her as she filled each glass at the tap. With all four glasses filled, she set them in front of the officer. As the woman held out a credit card, Callie scanned her olive skin and dark eyes.

"Want to start a tab?" Callie asked and accepted the payment.

"Yes, thanks."

Callie looked at the card. "Tina Ramirez. Nice to meet you."

"And you are?" Tina asked, giving Callie a small smile.

"Callie Mason." Callie turned to her register screen, tapped on it, and filed her card in a small box on the back counter.

"Let me know if you need anything," Callie said, returning a smile of her own, as the officer returned for the last two beers.

"Anything?" Tina teased.

Callie's smile widened, "I aim to please."

"I'll remember that," she said and walked back to her group.

As soon as Michael had the door to his apartment closed behind him, he pushed Alex up against the wall and covered her mouth with his. She felt his hands all over her body. It had been too long since she had been with anyone. She willingly gave into the feeling of being wanted. She felt Michael's need harden against her as he pressed himself into her stomach. She let him lead her into his bedroom where they quickly undressed and fumbled their way to the bed. Her breath caught as he entered her, and she moved slowly with him at first, and then faster. There was familiarity between them. They were quick, easy, and uncomplicated together.

"You feel so good," Michael groaned as he came and then made no move to separate himself from her. He propped himself above her to look at her.

Alex grinned and asked, "What?"

Michael's expression turned serious as he said, "I want you again."

Alex felt his sex fill inside of her, and her own yearning responded. She bit her lower lip and teased, "What are you going to do with that?"

Michael groaned and moved inside. He slid his hand between their bodies. He touched her purposefully, and she arched against him. She closed her eyes and her thoughts surprised her when they darted to Madison. As if in a slide show, she saw an image of Madison's body moving on the dance floor, then her amazing figure in the tailored suit standing in her office, then her dark blue eyes looking down at her, full of desire, about to put her mouth on her.

"Christ," she exhaled. Encouraging the fantasy, she continued to rub against Michael, urging him to stay right there. Until she came.

Buzzing from the alcohol and physically euphoric, Michael rolled off Alex onto his back. Alex, being too tired to go home yet, turned onto her side, curled up, and fell asleep. She woke before dawn and slipped out of Michael's apartment without waking him.

Chapter *Three*

Saturday

Alex opened the door to her house and whispered a hello to Kenzie and Moose, her four-year-old dogs. They were not fully awake, but they followed her upstairs anyway. She crawled back into bed with the hope of sleeping off more of her hangover. She woke a couple hours later to the soft whimpering sounds and pitter-patter of her four-legged companions circling her bed.

Alex had fond memories of the dogs she grew up with, so it seemed only natural to offer her home to these two in need of adoption several years ago. Her only reservation had been the fact that she was at work long hours of the day. Luckily, she had a retired neighbor who was more than willing to check in on them a couple times a day. The dogs were playing and wrestling around her as she dressed and made her way downstairs.

Alex started the coffee maker and opened the kitchen

door for the dogs. They tore off into the yard to take care of their morning business. In a matter of minutes, they were back, knowing that breakfast came next. They nudged her legs as she walked to the pantry for their food as if this would speed up the process. While the pups ate, she put on her paddock boots, bundled up in her favorite dark blue jacket and gloves, and threw her scarf around her neck before heading out the door.

The crisp February morning greeted her. She pulled her scarf tighter around her neck. The metal handle on the barn door was cold through her gloves. Simply crossing the threshold into the barn made her feel at peace. She loved the smell of freshly polished leather, the sweet aroma of the hay, and the sound of the horses as they moved around in their stalls. She walked through the tack room and her eyes landed on Dunkin's saddle perched on the wall. She noticed the farrier and hay bills stacked on her desk in the corner. She made a mental note to pay them later that day.

It also occurred to her that her boarder, Heather, had asked if she could bring some friends today to meet the horses and maybe ride. Heather said her friends were not used to being around horses, and she wanted to ease them into the experience. Alex thoroughly understood that and had told Heather that she did not mind at all. In preparation for the visitors, she tidied up the barn, working from one area to the next.

The horses stirred as they heard Alex moving toward them. Alex traveled from one horse to the next, greeting them with peppermints. They extended their heads through the opening of their stall doors to accept the refreshing treats. Alex relished the warmth of their breath on the palm of her hand. She walked across the center aisle to the hay room to collect a flake for each horse before preparing their breakfast grain.

Alex fed Dunkin first, her fifteen-year-old gray Percheron and Appaloosa mix. Alex had always been attracted to the grand size of draft horses, but because she also enjoyed riding, she needed a mixed breed to provide a gentle, relaxed ride. Alex moved to the next stall. Sterling was a bay, ten-year-old off-the-track thoroughbred. The remaining two occupied stalls were home to Max, an American Quarter Horse, and Cowboy, an American Paint Horse, both owned by her boarder, Heather.

While the horses ate, Alex returned to the house to enjoy her coffee. She took a seat at a well-worn farmhouse table overlooking the pasture and barn. She watched as the morning light through the windows caught the antique finish on the maple cabinets and the creamy tan tones on the granite countertops. She had been eager to renovate this space a year ago to make it her own. She enjoyed being surrounded by the original hardwood floors and the natural wood plank and beam ceilings throughout the home and loved the stone fireplace that blanketed one wall from floor to ceiling.

Her thoughts drifted to the previous night. Dinner had been a success. She had enjoyed her time with Michael. Heat rose on her cheeks as she remembered the part Madison played in the evening.

"Oh my god," she muttered to herself. It had been a long time since someone had stirred such feelings in her. It was throwing her off balance. Still, she couldn't help but grin to herself when she remembered her orgasm from the previous night. She allowed the feeling to linger while she finished her coffee and then headed back to the barn.

Alex led Dunkin from his stall to the wash stall, where he stood in the cross ties while she groomed him and put his tack on. She led him from the barn to the mounting block, mounted, and guided him down the path to the opening in the trees where the trail began.

It was calm and quiet except for a light breeze playing with the leaves on the trees. Alex and Dunkin moved through the wooded area and occasionally heard a squirrel rustling through the leaves for a stray nut here or there or a hawk calling out from a tree above them. In the stillness, Alex's thoughts returned to Madison. She was a sucker for a confident, intelligent woman in a business suit and something about Madison's presence made her weak in the knees. Not to mention how enticing her smooth voice was. She could listen to her talk all day long. And her captivating eyes seemed to stare a hole right through her. She had to make a mental note not to stare too long.

When the path approached the small stream running along the back side of the property, the trail widened and Alex asked Dunkin for a trot, which he happily gave. She pulled him back to a walk after a few yards and repeated this routine exercise until Dunkin's old bones were warmed up. He settled into a nice trot that required very little from Alex. She allowed the motion of his body to move hers up and then concentrated on directing her weight into the heel of her boots in order to make her body's return to the saddle as light and quiet as possible.

Over the years they had gained confidence in one another in finding this balance, the perfect timing of moving in unison. Alex's breathing fell in tune with Dunkin's as she felt his breaths beneath her. When they escaped the wooded path into the clearing, Alex sat deep in her seat, gave Dunkin more lead and asked for a canter. They moved across the ground in a rocking horse motion. Alex slowed Dunkin to a trot and then a walk as they traveled around the back of the covered arena until he had cooled down enough to bring him back in.

After Alex had returned Dunkin to his stall, she prepped Sterling for his round pen exercise. Like clockwork, she heard Heather pulling into the driveway. Moments later she heard women's voices and laughter. She stepped around Sterling as Heather walked into the barn and said hello.

"Hi, Heather," Alex greeted.

Heather jumped right into introductions as each woman entered the barn, "Alex, this is my college roommate, Rachel, in town visiting for the weekend. Beth, you've already met, and this is . . ."

"Madison," Alex said in a surprised voice, beating Heather's introduction. Alex ran her eyes over Madison, who looked absolutely adorable in her blue jeans, turtleneck, and light brown suede jacket. She had her hair down again, and it fell softly around her face.

Heather looked at Alex and then at Madison. "You two know each other?" she asked with a confused look on her face.

Madison said, "Actually, we just met recently." Heather still looked confused, and Madison added, "I'm working with Alex in a consulting capacity for her genetics project."

"Awesome," Heather said and smiled. When she led her friends over to the horses to make their introductions, Madison hung back.

She lowered her voice so only Alex could hear. "I'm sorry, Alex. I don't ever recall Heather sharing a name for who owned the barn she boarded her horses with. If you think this will make things uncomfortable, I totally understand, and I can leave."

Alex made eye contact and played it cool, "Don't be silly. I was just caught off guard when I saw you." *Yeah, because you had your way with me last night.* Alex blushed. "Please, go enjoy yourself today. I'm a little biased, but I think this is another good way to relieve stress." The reference to their conversation that had started weeks earlier wasn't lost on Madison, and she gave Alex a knowing look but didn't pursue it.

"Only if you are sure." The look on Alex's face confirmed her agreement, so Madison nodded and walked toward her friends.

What the fuck? Alex thought as she attempted to turn her attention to Sterling. She led him to the round pen and hooked him to the lunge line. *She shows up at my office and now here?* Alex asked Sterling for a walk, followed by a trot, and then a canter in a circle to the right around her, and repeated the exercise to her left. She reveled in his fluid motion and the sheer strength of his body.

Sterling was more than willing to please her. He seemed to enjoy the silent communication and connection with his person, and Alex thoroughly enjoyed this time with him and the sense of belonging it invoked. She was also fully aware that she was distracted. She kept looking over to where Heather and her friends were. More specifically to where Madison was. Heather was holding Max by his lead line, and her friends took turns riding him as she walked him around in circles. Madison's turn was after Rachel, and Alex watched her the whole time.

When his exercise workout was done, Alex walked Sterling back to his stall. She finished her routine by giving the horses another peppermint. *What beautiful and fantastic creatures*, she thought. She felt fortunate to have this private escape, never taking for granted what a special place this was. This is where she could detox from the rest of the world that could be so hurtful. Women's laughter coming from behind her pulled Alex from her drifting thoughts.

"We are headed out, Alex. Thank you," said Heather, and the other women chimed in similarly.

Madison added with a wave, "See you Monday."

"Yes, you will," Alex answered.

Chapter Four

Wednesday

Alex looked up from her computer when she heard her phone chirp. Madison's name flashed across the screen. She clicked on the text.

"Good morning, Alex. How are you?" Alex read.

Alex replied, "I'm well," and a smile tugged on the corners of her mouth. She added, "How are you?"

"Well, I have a light schedule today, and I was wondering if you might be free for lunch? I could stop by Judy's Deli and bring you an amazing, and I mean amazing, French bread sandwich."

Alex responded without hesitation, "My mouth is watering already. How does noon sound? That will give me a chance to finish up my morning meetings with the team."

"See you then."

She allowed her mind to settle on thoughts of

Madison for several minutes before she was back on task. She enjoyed reminding herself of how Madison looked at her the first time at the bar and how easy it had been for Madison to fit in here with her team. And now she could visualize Madison at her house and wondered how long she would be able to keep things between them strictly professional. The line was beginning to blur. The thought of something more between them excited her.

Alex returned her focus to her desktop and to the results from the latest time studies in preparation for her next readout to David and the grant committee. Her sister had always teased her about having a borderline obsessive-compulsive disorder because of how particular she was with just about everything. Alex laughed every time she heard it because she knew it was true. She was a planner, thrived on creating order from chaos, and liked her routine. She set high expectations for herself and for those around her. Most importantly, Alex enjoyed her work. The hours were long and grueling, but Alex thrived on the challenge of finding answers to questions and solutions to problems. She knew the upcoming months would be prove pivotal to the success of the research. The outcome of the tests would determine whether they got approved for the next wave of grants. Grants kept the research going. No grants, no research. She reviewed the time studies a third and final time.

As noon approached, Alex was caught off guard by how much she was looking forward to seeing Madison earlier than usual today. It was only an hour earlier, but they would be having lunch together for the first time and introducing personal time into their normal workday.

"What do you think? Alex?" Patricia repeated her question, and Alex was pulled away from her daydream.

"What, Patricia? I'm sorry."

"We aren't where we need to be yet. Our statistical results do not yield p-value < 0.05 for absolute certainty, but we are getting closer."

"Okay. Keep working at it."

Any other time Alex would have asked for details, but today all she really wanted to do was break for lunch. Patricia stared blankly at this uncharacteristic behavior as she watched Alex leave the room.

When Alex turned the corner to her office, she saw that Madison had already taken a seat on the couch and was organizing their lunch on the small coffee table. *She's taking care of me already*, Alex thought.

"Hi, Madison. Show me these amazing sandwiches. I'm famished." When Madison smiled at her, Alex realized that her attempt at a cool facade wasn't as armored as she had hoped. Her inner voice fired warning shots for her to stand down. *Would it really be that terrible to get to know her a little better?*

Madison had been right. The sandwiches were terrific, but Alex found her company to be more so. *What is it about this woman that draws me in?* Alex watched Madison while she spoke, absorbing how her slender fingers cradled her sandwich and how she wiped her mouth with her napkin after almost every bite.

Picking up the second half of her sandwich, Madison asked, "Where do you stand on the debate on whether or not we should have specific knowledge of our body's predisposition to disease through the use of genetic tests?"

"I am a scientist first and foremost, and I believe in the advancement of science. I see the benefit of genetic testing. It's reconstructing from within, not very different from the work of a cosmetic surgeon erasing a woman's facial wrinkles or removing the bags under her eyes. Women have breast implants and liposuction for all kinds of body parts they wish to change. Why not offer to do the same for potentially harmful genes? It begs the question for me, for example, if there would even be need of an organ transplant if we could re-engineer our DNA sequence to avoid certain outcomes. Medicinal and surgical therapy today combat pre-existing disease and existing conditions. But to advance to a state where we are able to preventatively alter those pre-existing conditions by protecting a person's DNA from virus and disease—well, that's true scientific discovery."

Playing devil's advocate, Madison asked, "What about Darwin's survival of the fittest theory and the natural evolution of the human race? It's a safety valve to avoid overpopulation in all species. We are supposed to die one day. Reengineering the natural course of our bodies seems to antagonize Darwin's theory and border somewhat on a God complex."

Alex chuckled and said, "If only it were that easy. Darwin's theory isn't going anywhere. The fittest bodies will still be required to fight off the disease, only in a different capacity. Their DNA will need to be strong enough to maintain the bond with the new molecular entity. If or when that bond weakens and releases its hold, the cells will, once again, be susceptible to disease."

Enjoying their sparring, Madison pushed on, "What about the humanity component? Not all women have the capacity or willingness to process information like this." Without giving Alex a chance to respond, she added, "And what about the decision between simply offering to test or making it part of a doctor's mandatory step protocol?"

Alex was more comfortable addressing the second option. "I believe the test should be mandatory, and patients with family history or preexisting conditions should be tested as early in adult life as possible. If one parent has the BRCA gene, their children have a fifty percent chance of also having it. If a woman has the mutation, her lifetime chance of getting the cancer jumps from thirteen to as high as eighty percent. Breast cancer can be aggressive. I think you could say it can even be irresponsibly aggressive. Prevention always trumps treatment in my book."

Madison had to prompt Alex for the first part of her question. "It's not that simple for everyone, Alex. Not all people are interested in that much information about themselves. Handing someone a potential life sentence before theirs has even begun is a heavy burden to carry, even for the very mature young lady."

Alex answered Madison's question with a question. "Why wouldn't people want to have time to get the proper prevention or appropriate treatment if necessary? People who know that they have a family history or know that they are pre-disposed to a disease state would be able to do something about it before it was too late. They would be given an opportunity to prevent disaster rather than wait until disaster occurs."

Madison said, "Let's use the analogy of reading a book and instead of reading from page one to the end, you skip over the middle and go right to the last page, just to see how it ends. A lot of people don't want to see how it ends. They would rather enjoy the journey, getting there with no expectations or preconceived ideas of how their journey will end. Doesn't skipping to the end take away some of our freedom of choice?"

"We aren't erasing the middle," Alex said. "We strive to make that journey more enjoyable for those who now suffer in pain with a medication that doesn't quite work or with a disease that reared its ugly head way too late to do anything about it. Having more knowledge enables us to be more successful at fighting disease. It helps us stay ahead of the curve. That knowledge is power."

"Knowledge can be crippling too. Ignorance is bliss, right?" Madison rebutted with a smile.

Showing some vulnerability, Alex admitted, "I may not fully relate to all those points of view, but I get it."

"Is our society really ready for this kind of control over our own existence?"

"I believe we are at the mercy of evolution, Madison. We must be ready," Alex said.

They ate in silence for a few reflective minutes before

Madison spoke up. "Well, you sure present a compelling case for scientific advancement, Alex. I assume debates such as this are what prompt opposing views and create the threats you and Michael mentioned?"

Alex nodded and said, "Exactly."

"What kind of threats are they?"

"They are usually in the form of letters or emails addressed to the office."

"Are they made toward you personally?"

"Sometimes they are directed to me or my team personally, yes." Alex made the statement almost stoically, and Madison felt a sudden urge to protect Alex.

"Doesn't that freak you out?"

"I understand that not everyone agrees with the work that we do here, and everyone is entitled to their beliefs and opinions. The threats have never escalated to more than written rhetoric and besides, Michael handles everything in that department, so I don't have to." Alex's voice trailed off.

Madison saw Alex's demeanor change and decided to stop the line of inquiry.

Their time together passed quickly. When one o'clock rolled around neither of them seemed to notice. Trevor tapped lightly on the door at the top of the hour.

"I lost track of time. I'm so sorry, Madison." Alex jumped up and began walking to the door.

"I'm not." Madison fell into step beside Alex as she led the way down the hallway and to the lab. "I wanted to ask you," she paused, suddenly seeming a little shy, reminding Alex of the night at the bar, "are you free for dinner

Friday night? I'm hosting a very casual get together with friends. I make a mean grilled steak and shrimp," she added, as if she had to sweeten the deal.

Instinctively, Alex was about to decline, but Madison's expression begged her to accept the invitation. She felt exposed, and it shook her. Madison read Alex's apprehension. She tilted her head and dramatically teased, "You do eat dinner, right?"

Their physical closeness, albeit in the middle of the hallway, made Alex catch her breath, and Madison's expression made Alex laugh. "Yes, of course I eat dinner."

"Around seven o'clock then? I'll text you my address."

Alex couldn't say no. She heard herself responding, "Sounds yummy. I look forward to it."

Friday

Alex arrived at Madison's apartment promptly at seven o'clock on Friday evening. It was located just on the outskirts of the city. The best of both worlds in her opinion, close enough to walk or grab the metro to immerse yourself in city life, but far enough away not to feel claustrophobic or closed in by the urban environment. Alex would have picked a similar location had she chosen to remain in the city. Madison buzzed Alex in through the outside entrance to her apartment building and opened her door with a welcoming smile as Alex was about to knock.

"I'm glad you could make it. Come in. Everyone's

in the kitchen." Alex followed Madison and saw three women standing around the kitchen island that was covered with plates of appetizers. Heather, Beth, and Rachel welcomed Alex in unison. She knew Heather and Beth, and after only a couple moments, she also recognized Rachel, Heather's friend and roommate from college.

"What would you like to drink?" Madison asked as she lightly touched Alex's back with the palm of her hand. Alex felt a shiver travel down her spine.

She scanned the island to see what everyone was drinking. "Red wine sounds good to me. Thank you."

Madison handed her a glass and waved her hand over the island. "Help yourself. Dinner will be ready in about twenty minutes."

When everyone drifted into the living room after dinner, Alex sat on the sofa as Madison headed toward a chair. Without thinking, Alex said, "You can sit over here. There's room." Alex started removing the throw pillows to make room between her and Rachel.

Madison said, "I'll take one of those. It's good for my back." When Madison got settled, Alex noticed Rachel lightly touch Madison's knee, and she caught a smile exchanged between them. She felt an unwelcome jolt in her gut. Still, Alex realized she was having more fun than she had in a long time. She was glad she had accepted the invitation. She was enjoying the moment and the company.

When Heather and Beth got up to leave around

ten o'clock, Alex decided she should leave with them. Alex watched as Madison gave everyone a hug goodbye. When it was her turn for a hug, Madison smiled and thanked Alex for coming. Madison's embrace was comforting and soft, and she held onto Alex for a couple of seconds before letting her go.

"Maybe you will get hungry sometime soon, and we can do this again," Madison said.

"If you're lucky." *I can't say no to her and now I'm flirting back. Shit.* She enjoyed that her response made Madison laugh.

"See you tomorrow." Heather was bringing Beth and Madison back to Alex's the following morning to ride the horses. Alex walked away with mixed emotions sparked from the pleasant sound of Madison's laugh and from the realization that Rachel wasn't leaving with the rest of them.

Saturday

Alex had downed her first cup of coffee and was in the middle of grooming Dunkin when she heard cars pull into the driveway. She moved toward the barn door to greet the women. Heather and Beth walked right to Max's stall. Madison followed Alex as she walked back to tend to Dunkin. Alex glanced at Madison as she stood there smiling at her. She secretly wondered if she showed everyone that beautiful smile and hoped that Madison saved it just for her. Her cheeks blushed at the thought.

"Are you going on a trail ride?" Madison asked.

"Yes."

"Do you want company?"

"I would love some," Alex couldn't help but smile back, "but what about Heather and Beth?"

"They want to stay in the ring today."

"Do you want to ride Dunkin?"

Madison took in a quick breath and said, "Sure, but I will tell you that I am stepping outside my comfort zone here. Last week was like the third time I've ever even been on a horse."

"Understood. I won't let anything bad happen to you," Alex said reassuringly.

"I'll hold you to that, Alex Bennett," Madison said, making Alex's insides do a somersault.

Heather led Max to the cross ties next to Dunkin to start the grooming process. As Alex began to groom Dunkin, Madison asked questions about what she was doing. Alex spent the next few minutes explaining the purpose of each step.

Madison secretly watched as Alex's riding breeches hugged her bottom when she bent to pick up one of Duncan's hooves to remove packed debris. Her fitted polo shirt slid up ever so slightly at the waistline and gave Madison a peek at Alex's bare back. Dark strands of her hair fell around her face. Alex's eyes lit up as she talked, and her smile was contagious. Madison could not help but smile back. Alex was comfortable in this environment, and Madison liked seeing this side of her.

Heather caught the way Madison stared at Alex.

When Alex bent down again, Heather got Madison's attention over Max's back and snickered, adding a little sideways shake of her head. Madison rolled her eyes.

"Now to the tack. The saddle pad goes on first, always from the left side," Alex said, demonstrating as she went. "You want to make sure you pull the saddle pad slightly away from the withers, so it doesn't pinch him. Then the saddle and girth," she said, as she swung the saddle onto his back and cinched up the girth.

"Where's the handle?" Madison asked.

"Sorry?"

"The handle that is supposed to be on the saddle. That you hold onto, like on Heather's."

"Oh, the saddle horn. Heather has a western saddle. This is an English saddle." Alex saw the worry spread on Madison's face.

"It's okay. I promise," Alex said. Madison hesitantly nodded.

Alex finished her tutorial by placing the reins over Dunkin's head, guiding the bit into his mouth, and gently pulling the crown piece over his ears. Before giving Madison a satisfied look, Alex fastened the neck and chin straps.

"You make that look easy," Madison remarked.

"It just takes practice."

When Alex walked away to get Sterling out of his stall, Heather whispered, "I have not seen you like this in forever, Madison. Are you flirting?"

"No. I'm not flirting," Madison retorted.

Alex pulled Sterling from his stall to get him ready to ride.

Outside, Alex guided the horses along the trails through the property and into the woods. It was cooler in the woods and a beautiful day. Knowing this was new to Madison, Alex kept the horses at a casual walk so she and Madison could comfortably talk while they rode.

Daring to enter new territory during a lull in their conversation, Madison said, "You and Michael seem close."

Madison seemed to have a knack for throwing Alex off guard. "Yeah, I guess so. We work well together."

After a short silence, Madison couldn't help but ask, "Are you dating him?"

"No. No, I work too much. I don't really date. No time for relationships," Alex replied evasively. Madison's thoughts returned to the night at the bar. She wondered if Alex's proposition was truly for a one-night stand because that was all she was interested in. Or maybe capable of? That made her uneasy.

"What about you?" Alex asked.

"What about me?" Madison asked.

"Are you dating anyone?"

"No, not at the moment."

Madison read confusion on Alex's expression, "What?"

"Sorry, it's just I thought you and Rachel were . . ." Alex's voice trailed off. She hoped Madison did not hear the slight annoyance in her voice.

"Why?" Madison asked.

"Last night at your apartment I saw Rachel touch your leg when we were sitting on the couch, and she stayed after the rest of us left."

Unaware and surprised that Alex was paying that much attention to their interactions, she explained, "We ended anything serious we had over two years ago. We have casually dated on and off since then."

Alex looked at Madison curiously and asked, "Are you on now?"

"No." Madison responded without hesitation. "So, you don't date ever?" she asked playfully. "As successful and beautiful as you are, I'd imagine you'd have a long line of men and women at your door."

"Sure, I mean, I go on dates," Alex felt the heat rise in her cheeks, "I just don't meet a lot of people who interest me enough that I'd want to date them repeatedly."

"Ah, so if it's someone you find interesting and they asked you out, you would say yes."

"Maybe," Alex teased. *I'd say yes if you asked me out.* "I mean, maybe, after I get through this project. It's difficult right now because I have to stay focused. When work is this crazy, I barely have time for my friends."

Alex's response gave Madison hope, and she kept it lighthearted, "Well, then I hope you will consider me a friend." She glanced at Alex and smiled.

After their ride was finished, they untacked the horses and returned them to their stalls. The four women walked out of the barn together.

Madison said, "Thank you for today, Alex. I had yet another good time with you." She gave her a quick hug and walked to her car.

"Friends have dinner together, right?" Madison asked

before closing the door.

Alex gave her a playful shrug and laughed.

Chapter
Five

Friday

Unwinding over drinks with a couple of her colleagues after a relentless week, Tina watched as Callie hugged and placed a kiss on the cheek of a pretty brunette. The look Callie gave the woman before she walked out of the bar was an intimate one. When Callie returned to her post behind the bar, Tina approached for another drink. She waited patiently until Callie noticed her.

"What can I get for you?" Callie asked.

"Well, I was going to ask for your number, but I just saw you walk your girlfriend out, so I guess I'll settle for a beer," said Tina through a cute grin.

"Hey, I remember you," Callie said. "My girlfriend?" Callie looked in the direction of the door and said, "Oh, Alex. Alex is a very good friend of mine, but she's not my girlfriend."

"Is there a girlfriend then?" Tina asked.

"No." Callie shot Tina a broad smile that could only be read as one of total interest.

Callie invited Tina to join her during her break to get acquainted. Once settled in a booth, Callie asked Tina to tell her about what it was like to be a cop, and Tina was interested in how Callie came to own and run a bar. They quickly fell into conversation about their parents, siblings, and the hometowns they each grew up in.

"How long have you and Alex been friends? You seem close," said Tina.

"Since our college days. Although I have to say, Alex was so much more devoted to school than I was. But it has paid off. She is going to find a cure for cancer." Callie's face beamed like a proud parent.

"Really? What kind?" asked Tina.

"Breast cancer." Callie's face was still beaming.

Tina's stomach lurched as if she had taken a punch to the gut. She tried to control her reaction. Lucky for her Callie stood, apologized about losing track of the time, and excused herself to get back to work. Callie fully intended to check back in with Tina later in the evening, but when she returned, Tina was nowhere to be found.

Tina was physically and mentally drained by the time she got home. She was unable to shake the feelings her conversation with Callie had provoked. What pissed her off the most was that she never saw it coming. She had scoped Callie as an easy lay. She owns a bar for fuck sake.

But to her surprise the woman had thrown a wrench in her plans.

She walked down the barren hallway to her bedroom, stripping out of her clothing as she went. She unlocked the gun safe stored in the bedside table to check for her personal firearm. Finding it there as usual, she put on the gray tank top and black shorts that had been piled in the chair.

She needed a drink. She rinsed out a dirty glass and poured herself two fingers of scotch from a bottle left on the counter from the night before. She downed it in one swallow and welcomed the numbing burn. She poured another and collapsed on the couch. Her eyes closed. In her mind's eye, Anne was standing in front of her, her expression forlorn.

"What's happened?" Tina asked.

"The doctor called back today," Anne said.

"And?"

"He wants me to get tested. He said because of my family history it would be a good idea." She started shaking.

Tina was at her side in an instant. She wrapped her arms around Anne's sagging shoulders and enveloped her, hoping her body would provide some solace.

"Sit down, let's talk through this."

"I watched my mom die of breast cancer." Anne's voice cracked and trailed off. "I can't go through what she did."

"Slow down, sweetheart. We don't know that you have breast cancer. He's merely suggesting you get tested for it, right?"

"Right." Anne's voice was weak. She looked exhausted.

"Do you want to get tested?"

"I don't know."

It dawned on Tina that with the recent double shifts she had volunteered for she had missed how this news and the possibilities were affecting Anne. Not knowing what to say, she didn't say anything and waited for Anne to speak again.

"My breasts make me feel like a woman, Tina. They make me feel sexy." Anne's gaze met Tina's. "I know you love them. You tell me that all the time. How would you possibly want me if I didn't have them?" Anne's question cut through Tina's heart like a knife.

"Honey," Tina leaned closer, choosing her words carefully, "yes, I love your breasts, but I love them because they are a part of you. I love all of you, and I will love you no matter what, always."

"But how could I ever feel whole without that part of me?" asked Anne.

Tina watched as Anne's gaze became distant. It chilled her to the bone. She felt Anne slipping away from her.

"What are you saying, Anne? Would it be easier for you not to know? To ignore what the doctor said?" Tina's voice tightened as she felt her own fear rising.

"You don't understand. How could you? You didn't have to watch the pain my mom endured going through a double mastectomy. And she still died. It was horrific, Tina," Anne shouted as her tears began to fall.

Tina knew Anne had lost her mother to breast cancer

when Anne was a teenager, but she didn't talk about it, ever. Tina drew in a deep breath to slow the pounding of her heart. This was no time for a panic attack of her own. She had to get a grip.

"What do you need me to do, Anne? How can I help you?"

"I don't know," Anne said through soft sobs. She clung to Tina with ferocity, her hands rhythmically clutching and then smoothing Tina's sweatshirt.

"If I have the test done and it's positive, will I be able to live with the what-ifs and the possibility it could happen to me? And if I don't have the test done, will the not knowing drive me crazy? Baby, this is an impossible decision for me."

"You don't need to make the decision tonight, and you're not alone in this." Tina smoothed Anne's hair as she spoke. "We can fight this together. I'm here for whatever you need from me. I will do whatever it takes." Her voice faltered. "Because I can't do here without you."

They sat entangled in each other's space for the rest of the evening, the heaviness of uncertainty surrounding them. Tina knew one thing with absolute certainty. Their lives were about to change in a big way.

Alex left Callie at the bar and arrived at Madison's apartment promptly at seven o'clock. Madison had casually brought up the friendly dinner conversation again with Alex midweek. Anticipating the question this time, Alex had accepted without hesitation. She reached for the doorbell. *Friends having dinner. That's all this is*, she reminded herself.

Madison answered the intercom seconds after Alex rang the doorbell. "Come on up, Alex."

Alex found Madison's apartment door ajar this time, and she let herself in. She was greeted with the smell of home cooking, a warm and inviting aroma that always seemed to invoke the feeling of the holidays for Alex. She was immediately put at ease, and her heart fluttered in her chest. Madison met her in the living room with a huge smile and gave her a hug hello. *God, her body feels good.* She looked comfortable in her khakis and a soft, white, button-down blouse that hung intimately on her frame.

"Here, I brought you some wine. Red and white since I don't know which you like better."

"Well, I do enjoy red more, but I don't discriminate," Madison said with a wink. Alex's insides did a somersault. "Come on in. Feel free to look around while I finish dinner. It occurred to me that last time I never gave you a tour. Sorry about that."

"No worries. What can I do to help?

"Go relax. I've got this covered." Alex hesitated. "Show yourself around. Really," Madison insisted.

Madison took the wine from Alex and headed back into the kitchen. Alex moved around the living room, taking in everything. The room was tastefully decorated with stunning pieces of furniture including a gorgeous antique table, all facing a rough stone fireplace and mantle. She studied the pictures on the mantle.

"Are all these pictures of your family?"

"Yes, my parents are in the picture with me and my brother and sister are in the beach pictures."

"They are beautiful," Alex said and noticed that in all the pictures the figures were touching in some way. Arms around each other or hooked together, a hand on a shoulder, or laced around a waist. The physical display of genuine affection caused another flutter in her chest. A whole family. A complete family.

"Thank you," Madison responded from the kitchen.

Alex continued her tour down the hallway and found two bedrooms, each with an on-suite bath. The bedroom on the left was Madison's. She decided not to go in, not wanting to intrude in her private space. The room on the right was an office with a handsome wooden desk in the middle of the floor and a couple piles of paperwork scattered around a laptop computer. *Work in progress,* Alex guessed. Alex made her way back toward the kitchen and found Madison preparing a salad.

The kitchen was very bright and inviting. The apartment was at the rear of the building and allowed for a small outside patio with access directly from the kitchen. Alex poked her head out to see just enough space for a grill, a small table, and two chairs. Past the kitchen was the dining room with seating for six. The table was already set. Madison came in carrying the salad.

"How long have you lived here?" Alex asked as she seated herself at the table.

"About seven years."

"It's very nice."

"I like it. Do you have any siblings other than Amber?

"No, it's just the two of us."

"Amber lives here in the city, right?

"Yes, both my sister and my mom live in the city."

"Are you close to your family?"

"We're closer now that we are all adults. I was always so focused on school and my career I usually had my head in a book instead of spending time with people," Alex explained.

"Where does your dad live?"

"He died in a construction accident when I was young."

"I'm so sorry for your loss, Alex."

"Thank you. It was a long time ago, and we survived." She usually stopped there but something in Madison's expression compelled her to continue.

"Amber and I grew up an un-extraordinary, middle-class town in southeastern Maryland. Dad worked with large, commercial construction equipment. One day, while they were using the crane to place metal beams for the foundation of an apartment building, the main power cable snapped. The operator lost control of the crane's arm, and it struck my dad in the head. They said he was killed instantly. I was sixteen and Amber was twenty. We struggled for some time after that. Mom picked up a second job to make ends meet."

Alex reflected for a moment. "I've always admired Mom for her strength, but most of all for her endless reserve of optimism and selflessness. She would say things like, 'One day at a time, Alex, that's all you can do' or 'We'll just rob Peter to pay Paul, he won't mind.' I asked her once how she kept going, how she kept pressing on when faced with one setback after another. She said, 'You either get over it or you go around it, but regardless, you keep moving forward, and you never give up.' So, I immersed myself in my studies both in high school and college to keep myself moving forward."

Wanting to ease the look on Alex's face, Madison redirected the conversation, "How did you get into genetics?"

"I was drawn to genetics around the time I learned about pharmacogenetics and the effects of medications on the body's DNA gene sequences. It's a challenge to find ways to stunt disease. I thrive on solving complicated problems. Developing molecules that can bind to a gene mutation and halt its negative action isn't easy. Our attempts have been repeatedly met with failure. Our synthetic variations have only worked short term, as you now know.

"I want to be able to re-engineer our healthcare system and transition it from a treatment-centric model to a prevention-centric model. One where we can identify the genes most predisposed and susceptible to disease and target them for prevention therapy before the disease has a chance to start taking over the good cells. We're still years from this becoming a medical standard, but it's exciting nonetheless. Well, at least in my opinion."

"It is fascinating work, Alex. Truly. I've been interested in gene therapy, especially for breast cancer, ever since my aunt was diagnosed with breast cancer five years ago and beat it."

"I'm so glad to hear she's a survivor," Alex responded. "I'm really hopeful that one day our work will help many more women a lot sooner who are in the same situation."

"Here's to that." Madison raised her wine glass to toast. Alex raised her glass to meet Madison's and as the clink of the glass faded, Madison stood and said, "Leave the dishes. I'll clean them up later."

Madison turned on the gas fireplace in the living room with a flip of a switch, and as they settled on the couch, Alex said, "So what about you? You have a brother and sister. Where do you fall in the mix?"

"Right in the middle. My brother, Derrick, is two years older and my sister, Sutton, is three years younger."

"Do they live nearby? I get the impression you are close," said Alex and motioned to the photos.

"Yes. Both of my siblings live within an hour of here. We try to get together monthly, but sometimes it's two months before we see each other."

"What do they do?"

"They're both dentists. My dad is also a dentist, and my mom is a dental hygienist, so they were thrilled my siblings followed suit. It was their first choice for me too, but they are so supportive that it didn't matter what profession I chose."

Alex felt a warm flush wash over her. She attributed it to the wine at first, but then decided it was the physical pull to Madison that she was reluctantly resisting. Madison used her hands as she spoke, occasionally touching Alex's arm or leg for effect. The repeated touches were sending nervous impulses back and forth to her brain. Alex studied Madison as she spoke. Her eyes appeared darker in the firelight and were framed with long mascara-enhanced eyelashes. The outline of her lip pencil darkened as her lipstick wore away from their evening of eating and drinking. *Shit. She caught me staring at her mouth.* Madison had stopped talking. The silence was maddening.

Intrigued, Alex asked, "What are you thinking?"

"Honestly?" Alex thought she saw desire in Madison's eyes. Alex nodded and waited for her answer. Madison ran her slender fingers through her hair and tucked a few strands behind her ear. Alex resisted another urge to touch her.

Madison had never been good with keeping her feelings to herself, but she hesitated, afraid she might scare Alex off, so she answered with an honest response, just not the one from mere moments before.

"I am incredibly attracted to you." Alex sat up straighter, Madison's fear was confirmed, and she quickly added, "I'm sorry. I didn't mean to make you uncomfortable."

"You didn't. I mean, you do make me uncomfortable but not in a bad way," Alex blurted out and took a gulp of her wine to calm her nerves. *Shit's getting real now. Time to deflect.*

After a second gulp, Alex's voice was flat, "I thought you weren't interested."

"Why do you say that?"

"Because of the night at the bar."

"What were you expecting?" Madison was aware that the sensible thing to do was to keep her attraction for

Alex in check, especially if she convinced herself that Alex wasn't capable of handling anything more than a fling. Even though it had not been what Madison had wanted to hear, Alex had been clear about not wanting to date and having no time for a relationship. Battling those two things was a heartache waiting to happen.

"Honestly?"

"Please."

"I thought you were going to ask me back to your place."

Madison snickered, "Well, that would have made Rachel happy."

"Sorry?"

"She goaded me into approaching you, thinking some flirting would do me good and if it ended in a one-night stand, even better. To quote Rachel, I 'needed to work off my bitchy edge.'"

"And you obviously didn't fully agree with that," Alex said, not having been privy to anything remotely bitchy about her.

"Full disclosure, I'm not good at one-night stands. They get too messy for me."

Alex didn't say anything but slowly nodded and absently chewed on her bottom lip.

"What about you?" asked Madison softly. She was afraid of what the answer might be, but she needed confirmation nonetheless.

"What about me?"

"How do you feel? About casual sexual partners, I mean."

Alex's eyes searched the room as if she would find the right words hanging in the air around them.

While Alex deliberated, Madison added, "To be honest, you confuse me. That night at the bar, you were so confident, bold, and so sure of yourself, but sitting here, I tell you I'm attracted to you and you seem shy."

Time to come clean. Alex straightened and said, "I'm not proud of what I'm about to say."

Madison was tuned in and hanging on every word.

"There are only two places where I am totally comfortable in my relationships. One is my lab, doing the research that I love and two is like at the bar having fun with no strings attached."

Alex watched Madison's expression fall into one of disappointment and quickly added, "Because I suck at relationships."

"So, work aside, you are only comfortable in social situations where you don't have to invest yourself and you have nothing to lose."

"Well, hearing it out loud like that makes me sound callous, but, yes, I guess you are right."

"Someone that unfeeling and uncaring could never do the work you do, Alex." Madison shook her head. "No, I think there's more to it than that." Madison regarded Alex as if trying to solve a puzzle.

"You let me know when you have me figured out. I'll take any help I can get." Alex laughed in a feeble attempt to lighten the mood. "What happened with Rachel? If you don't mind me asking."

Seemingly unfazed with the subject change, Madison

eyes softened, "Our timing was off. We simply did not want the same things at the same time."

"I get that," Alex said, but did not elaborate.

"In what way?"

"The priorities being different part," Alex said, recalling a particular day from her past.

Madison kept probing, her curiosity getting the better of her, "What was his name, her name?"

Alex dropped her gaze to her wine glass resting in her lap. "Her name was Kate."

"Did you love her?"

Alex slowly traced the rim of her glass with a finger. "Yes, I did love her in my own way."

"How long ago was this?" Madison asked, her curiosity transforming into need.

"A lifetime ago." Alex took a deep breath and looked at her watch. "It is getting late. I should go." Alex abruptly set her wine glass on the coffee table and stood.

Madison reached for Alex's arm, "Alex, I am sorry. I didn't mean to pry. I just . . ."

"It's okay," Alex said, retreating to a safe place. "I'm not good at this."

"What do you mean by 'this'?"

"Opening up, sharing my feelings, letting people in."

"But I sense you want to let me in."

"Yes. Yes, I do. It's just so hard for me."

Madison was standing so close Alex closed her eyes and savored the absolutely delicious mixture of perfume and shampoo she now associated with only Madison. It made her nerve endings tingle, and she wanted so desperately to kiss Madison. She had to resist the urge to lean in and take what she wanted. It wouldn't be fair to take advantage of what Madison was offering, especially if Alex bailed on her later. Confusion was all Alex could manage right now except for the fact that hurting Madison would be unbearable. Needing some kind of contact, Alex settled for Madison's hands and reached out for her. Madison immediately responded and their fingers entwined.

"It's okay. These things take time, and I'm not in any hurry." Madison's voice was soft and caressing.

Alex pulled her hands away and said, "Thank you for dinner and tonight. See you tomorrow?"

"I'll be there."

Saturday

Alex woke to the familiar feeling of serenity for the day ahead. It was Saturday. As sleep faded and her consciousness brought her into the full light of day, an anxious nervousness joined her usual state. Madison was coming today. Their evening flooded back to her, causing a tingling sensation to run through her. She had to admit that she wanted to see Madison, although truth be told, she was fearful to even consider opening up to someone again.

Deep down she wanted a significant other in her life, but at what cost? What she had been able to give to Kate wasn't enough. But she had learned that giving everything was too painful, and she couldn't bear the thought of that black hole again. She had barely survived it. Callie's voice echoed in her mind. "I'm getting ahead of myself again. Madison admitted to being attracted to me. That's all," Alex said, half out loud and let out a deep breath. *And I'm attracted to her too, but God help me, I know it's leading to more than that.*

Nothing good came from ruminating. During their conversation last evening, Madison had asked Alex if she would give her a riding lesson. Her previous couple of experiences were during vacation excursions but nothing formal. Alex's plan was to keep to the lesson unless Madison brought up their conversation. *You are such a coward.*

Alex watched as Madison took the three steps up the mounting block, grabbed the reins, and swung her right leg over Dunkin's back with ease. Madison enjoyed running and yoga, disciplines facilitating good balance and core strength, both of which were advantageous to horseback riding. Alex led horse and rider away from the barn and into an open space where they could walk around without any obstacles in their way. Alex stepped back to assess Madison's seat and leg position.

"The stirrups are too long. Let's try shortening them by two holes."

She removed Madison's foot from the stirrup and gently pushed her leg up and forward. Madison felt a jolt through her boot like a shock from an electric fence. The feeling was reinforced when Alex guided Madison's foot back into the adjusted stirrup.

She silently watched Alex as she adjusted the iron. When she asked her how it felt, Madison was unable to answer. She just nodded. Alex moved to the other side and repeated the process. Madison braced for the contact the second time. It affected her the same way, but she tried to ignore it.

"Anything in particular you'd like to know about riding?"

"I've never been given a lesson, so anything you share will be new to me. Start at the beginning, I guess."

Alex thought for a moment and recalled one of her early riding experiences. "How about if we start with the horse then?" Madison nodded.

Alex explained to Madison how to affect Dunkin's movements by turning his head, neck, and shoulder with the bit and reins, viewing them as extensions of her arms, and by guiding his barrel with her legs through a turn.

"When you apply that pressure on his belly, his hindquarters will follow, and he won't fall into the center."

Alex asked Madison to sit up straight and relax her arms at the elbows with her hands rested at the withers.

"Pull your shoulders back and relax through your thighs and knees and let your weight fall into your heels."

"That's a lot to think about all at once," said Madison.

Alex nodded. "Are you okay? How do you feel?"

"This feels more balanced now, more comfortable."

"Go ahead and ask him for a bigger walk by nudging him with both feet. Very nice. Keep his head straight in the direction you are moving by alternating left rein, right rein with a subtle squeeze of your hands on the bit. If he leans too far left or right, use your inside leg, from the knee down, to build a wall so to speak, against his barrel. As you apply pressure, he will move away from it. Once he is straight again, release the pressure. This teaches him through positive reinforcement. Let's change direction and ask him for another forward walk. Nice." Madison was listening intently and following Alex's commands without saying a word.

Alex continued, "Horses are amazing animals. They cannot understand full sentences, but they can understand short commands, and they can sense how we feel. They can mirror our emotions and teach us to understand ourselves better, if we pay attention and listen to them."

"How do you mean?" Madison asked.

"I was struggling with one of my horses years ago. I brought it up with my trainer at the time, and she asked me how I felt. I didn't understand what she was asking. She told me that my horse was simply mirroring or acting out the conflicting feelings coming from me. She asked me what was going on, and I told her that I was going through a rough patch at work."

Madison stopped Dunkin in front of Alex as she continued with her story. "My trainer suggested that I identify my emotions and practice owning them one hundred percent. She said I didn't need to pretend they weren't there. She asked me to try to avoid letting my mind block the emotions or to try to talk myself out of feeling a certain way. It was times like these, she said, that I was confusing my horse, and he didn't know how to show up for me.

"I started practicing by stating out loud how I felt, more for my sake than his, but it started working. He started acting out less around me. I realized that it had never been him at all. He was just reflecting my conflict back at me, and once I became aware of it, and corrected it, his behavior changed. He remained calm for me regardless of the type of emotions I felt as long as I allowed myself to feel them completely and own them."

Madison was fascinated by the theory of horses teaching emotional agility, mesmerized by the passionate look on Alex's face as she told her story, and attracted to her vulnerability in sharing such a personal experience.

Alex grinned and said, "Enough of my stories for one day."

Alex would make a great instructor, Madison thought. *She's extremely knowledgeable and so calm. Her verbal cues made it feel natural to do what she asked.*

"Thank you for sharing the story with me," Madison said. She opened her mouth to say more but changed her mind.

Alex's grin turned into a pleased smile. "Well, thank you for making me feel comfortable enough to share."

They finished in the barn, and Alex walked Madison to her car.

"I wanted to apologize for last night," Madison said suddenly.

"You don't need to apologize."

"Yes, I do. I shouldn't have pried." Madison searched for the right words. "I got caught up in the moment, had too much wine, and I said too much. I was pushy and I'm sorry."

Alex's voice was low and husky, "Don't ever be sorry for telling me how you feel about me." She cleared her throat and added, "Besides, I'm the one who should apologize. I'm the one with the total obsession with my research and the fucked-up psyche." She forced a laugh.

"So, we are okay?" Madison waved her finger back and forth between them.

"We are okay."

"Good. I'll see you Monday," Madison said as she drew Alex closer to give her a goodbye hug.

Chapter *Six*

Friday

The week came and went without any real success. Alex and her team were disappointed because the MMH molecule would not bind to the DNA gene strand for longer than thirty minutes, not long enough for a sustained therapeutic effect, so their long-awaited breakthrough was not ready. Alex told Patricia to tell the others to start their weekend early and to get some rest so they could tackle it again, refreshed, on Monday.

Exhausted, Alex stopped by the bar to see Callie on her way home. Callie greeted her in their usual booth with drinks and an appetizer. She placed her bounty on the table, wrapped her arm around Alex's shoulder, and leaned over to place a kiss on the top of her head before taking a seat across from her.

"So, let's hear it."

Alex forced a smile and filled her in on her

non-progress with her research.

"And where are we with Mad-i-son?" she asked, slowly drawing out the name as she said it. "I want all the details."

Alex appreciated the way her friend always included herself in the story, as if they were both moving through experiences in tandem. It kept her grounded.

"Remember a few weeks ago when I went home with Michael?"

"Of course."

"Well, I haven't shared the whole evening with you." Alex knew that her attraction to Michael was purely physical, and she had nothing to feel guilty about, but she still did. Callie anxiously leaned toward Alex.

"While we were, you know," Alex grinned, "I was thinking about Madison."

Callie leaned back and laughed. "Oh my god, that's awesome!"

Alex disagreed and rambled, "It's not awesome. I told her I only have time for friends and that I don't date and that I'm not looking for a relationship right now because I have to stay focused on my work. I can't seem to form real sentences around her unless I stick to the work stuff. Otherwise, I become a blabbering idiot."

"Am I hearing confirmation received then? She's into you?" Callie asked and Alex nodded.

"I'm glad to hear you're getting somewhere because when I asked Amber, she claimed that she didn't know much about her personally."

"You really called Amber?" Alex raised her eyebrows in disbelief.

"Yes, of course I did. Don't act like you didn't know I would. But never mind that. What did you two talk about?"

"I asked about Rachel, from her party, and she told me they were together a couple years ago."

Callie's eyes widened. "And then you said you only have time to be friends." Callie wasn't surprised. "Alex, oh Alex, this is what you do every time there is a hint of something more than just physical attraction. You are over analyzing and fast-forwarding at warp speed again, babe. You cannot control this, so don't even try. You don't need to figure out what comes next. Just focus on right here, right now, okay?"

"Honestly, Callie? Right here, right now is getting old. It's not as fulfilling as it used to be. What if I *am* ready for more? What if this time would be different? How will I know?"

"It is not magic, but you just know. You like her, yes?" Alex nodded. "You *really* like her?" Again, Alex nodded. "Then you should talk to her and find out what she wants. It's not about finding someone you can live with. It's about finding someone you simply cannot live without." Callie acted out the last few words as if reading from a movie script, trying unsuccessfully to make Alex laugh.

Alex exhaled and said, "I did have that feeling once. I was young and scared and stupid, and I let her walk away. With all the feelings Madison is stirring up, I can't stop thinking about how terrible I was to Kate. Maybe I just don't have the capacity to be with someone like that."

"There is nothing wrong with you, Alex. You simply weren't ready for what Kate was offering, but you are definitely drawn to this Madison woman. There's no set timetable with this stuff, Alex. It's an individual journey we take at our own pace."

"If I'm honest with myself, I think you are right. Instead of dealing with my insecurities and fears, I avoid them by focusing my attention on my work." Alex shook her head slowly.

Callie changed the subject. "I have some news too. A really cute cop asked me out."

"What cop?"

"Her name is Tina Ramirez. She's been coming in to grab a drink after work over the last couple weeks."

"What do you know about her?"

"She's single. She's been a cop for three years, comes from a family of cops, and moved here recently when she was assigned to a local district."

"You're acting weird. What is it?"

"She just intrigues me, that's all. She has a dark edginess about her that I find attractive."

"If I didn't know any better, I'd say you want to do more than just sleep with her." Seeing the look on Callie's face, Alex gasped. "Really? I don't know who you are right now."

Callie raised her glass and toasted, "Here's to trying new things."

They both drank, laughed, and devoured their appetizers.

Wednesday

Another grueling work week began but yielded no better results than the previous one had. Alex joined Patricia and Madison in the conference room. Patricia looked physically distressed as she manipulated the 3D computer image hovering above them. Alex asked her to try a different way, yielding yet another unsuccessful outcome. They kept trying different iterations with the 3D rendering of the molecules and gene sequences with no success. Alex quietly looked back and forth between the 3D rendering and the data splayed out on the table in front of her and processed her thoughts out loud.

"Let's think about this. Basic pharmacology tells us that Tamoxifen is an antagonist of the estrogen hormone receptor. That's why it's so effective in the treatment of breast cancer. By blocking the hormone receptor, it reduces the levels of the estrogen hormone that stimulates the growth of the tumor."

"True, it is a competitive antagonist," added Madison.

Alex had an idea. "Patricia, our primary focus has been creating a hybrid of the Tamoxifen molecule that will bind directly to the mutated gene. What if we create a way to anchor an estrogen hormone receptor to the mutated gene sequence? We already know MMH will bind to that. It would, in theory, inactivate the gene mutation and add a preventative measure to make certain any potential pre-existing growth is stunted, right?"

"A DNA strand that includes the estrogen hormone

receptor . . . yes, Alex, that's definitely worth a try. I'll get the team started on the modeling right away."

Alex was as disappointed as Patricia with their current results even knowing full well this was par for the course in the world of medical research. You try and try again and keep working toward that particular day when that day's effort makes all the difference, a culmination of all the days preceding it. Alex and Madison walked out of the lab together.

"How are you, Alex? You look tired," Madison said with a worried look on her face.

Alex shrugged it off. "It comes with the job." She looked at Madison for a moment and out of the blue asked, "Have you ever been to a horse show?"

Madison's worried expression transformed into one of surprise, "No, I haven't."

Here's to trying new things, Callie had said. Needing some refueling time and before losing her nerve, Alex blurted out, "Would you like to go with me this weekend? There's a show three and a half hours away. We'd leave Friday night and be back late Sunday afternoon."

Madison smiled, "What time should I be ready?"

Friday

Alex checked them into their hotel Friday evening at nine-thirty. The receptionist handed a room key to Alex and then one to Madison. They rode the elevator to the same floor and arrived at their rooms, finding them adjacent to one another.

Odd, thought Madison. When she traveled with colleagues, hotels always seemed to place them on different floors.

They were each about to swipe their keys when Alex realized what had happened. *Clever, Trevor.*

"Did you book these rooms?" Madison asked as her door panel lit up green and beeped.

"Trevor," Alex said.

"Hmm. Night." Madison stepped into her room and closed the door.

"Good night," Alex said as Madison's door was closing.

Saturday

When Alex and Madison arrived at Lakehouse Wood Farms about half-past eight the next morning, the place was buzzing with activity. They followed directional signs until a young man wearing an orange vest waved them into a parking spot. The fenced-lined pasture facing them had been repurposed for the day to accommodate the visiting horse trailers. There were more than thirty trailers parked there already. Most of the horses were tied next to their trailers and eating hay. Spectators and riders, some fully dressed in their competition gear and some in their day-to-day riding outfits, were walking around the grounds.

Hearing an announcement that the cross-country trials were about to start, Alex and Madison located a gate displaying a "Cross Country Enter Here" sign and followed a worn path to a set of bleachers. They found seats at the far end of the crowded bleachers. Alex secretly enjoyed having Madison in her personal space. Their legs touched and Madison didn't pull away from the contact. The closeness made it easy for Alex to touch her knee or lean in as they held conversation.

For the next hour and a half, they watched eventers from various divisions. Alex explained that divisions separated the competitors by each course's degree of difficulty. The program began with the more seasoned riders competing in the Training Division and then continued through the Novice, Beginner Novice, Maiden, and finally Green as Grass levels. The announcer would broadcast when a horse and rider cleared all their jumps or when a horse and rider refused one.

After half the cross-country event concluded, Alex and Madison made their way to the Dressage arena. They saw five riders in the warm-up area. One rider was finishing her routine and the next rider made her way around the outside of the ring in preparation to enter. Her horse was a beautiful off-the-track thoroughbred with a shiny black coat and a braided mane and tail. He pranced into the ring as if he understood it was his turn to show off what he knew. The communication between horse and rider was very evident. The spectators showed their appreciation of the fine performance with enthusiastic applause.

A hush fell over the crowd as each new competitor entered the ring. Alex enjoyed this event even more than the cross country because Madison was whispering her questions in Alex's ear. Which meant she had to get even closer to be heard. Alex took advantage of the opportunity to study Madison's face as she watched the event and unabashedly watch her lips as she would mouth things to her to avoid being a distraction. She felt a tingling sensation course through her every time Madison looked over at her or smiled at her. It warmed Alex to see Madison join in with the rest of the spectators, reacting when the crowd noticed a mistake or clapping after each completed routine.

Alex and Madison moved on to the food trucks for something to eat and drink before finishing the day watching the jump events. Alex watched Madison devour the chili cheese dog she had ordered. She was overcome by a warm wave of emotion. It was like feeling infatuation, peace, and home all rolled up into one. And it made her long for something more in her life.

Madison caught Alex staring at her with an expression that she couldn't quite place. With a mouth full of chili dog, she asked, "What?"

"I don't know. You just seem to have it together all the time and you seem so reserved, I never expected you to be okay with eating a messy hot dog from a food truck."

Looking around them as she swallowed, Madison said, "Well, you didn't give me a lot of choices here, and I'm hungry." She licked her lips and wiped her mouth with a clean corner of her napkin. She grinned and a wave of embarrassment washed over her face.

"You're adorable. I like it." *I like you*, Alex admitted to herself. "So, I take it I need to do a better job with dinner then?" Alex asked, hoping she'd say yes.

"Yes, you do," Madison answered teasingly. Her smile made her eyes twinkle and the matter of fact tone of her voice made Alex's stomach flip.

Alex picked a restaurant on the drive back to the hotel. Feeling compelled to give Madison an opportunity to back out, she asked, "Are you sure you're not tired of me yet?"

Madison shook her head with a laugh, "Not yet."

Alex had enjoyed the ease of their time together through the day, and dinner was no exception. Being with Madison was comfortable and felt like spending time with an old friend. It was in this familiarity in their interactions during these normal, seemingly uneventful moments that wanting Madison's undivided attention became crushingly apparent to her.

They returned to the hotel, said their goodnights, and retired to their own rooms. Alex paced around her room, still keyed up from the day they had shared. Knowing it was a risky idea but not able to stop herself, Alex knocked on the door adjoining their rooms and invited Madison to her room for another glass of wine.

"Cheers."

"Cheers," Madison repeated and took a sip of wine, without taking her gaze from Alex. They sank into some pillows they repurposed onto the small couch in the room.

"Did you have a good time today?" asked Alex.

"I did. Gives me so much more appreciation for the riders and horses after watching the different disciplines, not to mention how much planning and preparation must go into pulling off these events."

"I'm glad you liked it."

Madison paused and her voice lowered, "I liked your company today too."

"Me too," said Alex. "Yours I mean."

"I admit you still confuse me, Alex."

"Why?"

Madison's tone was serious, "I think you know the answer to that."

"Please tell me."

"The way you acted with me today, honestly, felt more like a date to me. And the way you are looking at me right now is telling me you want something more than a friend would give you. You flirt with me and then you withdraw. I feel something happening between us. Am I completely misreading this?"

Alex's mouth went dry, and her heart hammered at Madison's directness and her comfort level and willingness to openly discuss such things. Alex had very little practice admitting to herself what she wanted from others, let alone saying it out loud. The fact that Madison could read her so easily made her feel naked and exposed. She opened her mouth to respond, but she couldn't find the words. She looked at Madison, desperately wanting her to understand.

Madison was moved by the look of panic on Alex's face. "What is it? You can tell me," she said.

Alex shook her head, "I don't know how."

"It's okay. Come here." Madison put her arm around Alex's shoulder.

Welcoming the numbing affect the alcohol had on the over-protective voice in her head, Alex cautiously leaned into Madison. After a few moments, Alex relaxed against her. Surprised, Madison leaned back against the cushions. Alex stretched alongside Madison until she could feel the full length of Madison's body against her own. She wrapped her arms around Madison's waist and nestled her face into her hair and neck. Alex had long ago locked away her craving for this kind of connection, but lying here now, that door swung wide open and she tightened her hold as if her life depended on it. The emotions from earlier in the day crashed over her again, sending a warm rush through her. *She feels like home*, Alex admitted to herself.

"I'm afraid," Alex said in an exhale that was barely more than a whisper.

"Don't you think this is scary for me too?"

Madison tilted Alex's face up to look at her. She tucked a strand of Alex's hair behind her ear. The desire in Alex's gaze weakened her defenses. She bent and lightly kissed Alex's neck. When her lips traveled to her ear, Alex shivered. Madison fully expected Alex to pull away, but she didn't. Madison slowly placed tiny kisses along Alex's chin as she made her way to the corner of

Alex's mouth. She lingered there a second before placing a tentative kiss on Alex's lips. She waited for Alex to respond. When Alex did respond, she did so like she was suffocating, and Madison was pure oxygen.

Alex immediately yielded to the pressure of Madison's lips. Their tongues began a playful interaction of asking and answering as they slid back and forth and around each other. Madison deepened their kiss and wrapped her arms around Alex's waist to pull her closer. The combination of Alex's soft curves and toned body stirred an ache deep in her belly and she felt her pulse quicken.

Madison ignored her internal struggle and whispered into Alex's mouth, "You feel so good."

Alex's body trembled again. "You have no idea."

Alex traced her hand along Madison's back from her shoulder blade to her waist and heard Madison let out a small sigh. Her reaction urged Alex on, and she moved her hands down Madison's side, over her hips and to the back pockets of her jeans. When Alex's hand traveled over Madison's backside to between her legs, Madison sighed again. Alex pulled Madison's leg on top of her own, nestling herself between Madison's thighs.

The overwhelming heat traveling through Madison's jeans as Alex pressed herself against her core ignited Alex's desire even more. She craved the feel of skin on skin. Alex greedily pushed aside Madison's top to run her hand across Madison's waistline, wanting to thoroughly savor everything warm and inviting about her. Madison moaned when Alex ran her hand over her breast and squeezed her taut nipple through the fabric of her bra. Blindsided, the thought of losing control crashed over Alex. Her body went rigid.

Sensing the change, Madison tilted her head back and whispered roughly, "If we don't stop now, I won't want to. We've had a lot to drink, and I don't think we want our first time together to be a drunken mess." Almost regretfully, she laughed, "God help me, I imagine this would be an absolutely amazing mess, but I want our first time together to be something you choose to do when you are fully aware of what you are doing."

Agreeing whole heartedly, Alex whispered, "I don't want to hurt you."

"What do you mean?" asked Madison.

"I want you, Madison. It's the emotions I don't know what to do with."

Madison nodded and reluctantly pulled herself away. *So close and yet so far away. Alex really was a heartache waiting to happen.* She walked out of the room without another word. She closed the door between their rooms softly. Alex heard the click as Madison engaged the lock.

Alex stripped down to her underwear and crawled into bed. She was exhausted from her mental sparring, but her unfulfilled desire from their encounter wouldn't let her fall asleep. She couldn't stop thinking about Madison lying in the next room. *Is she asleep yet? Is she thinking about me?* She lay there awake, replaying their kissing and touching. The thought of wanting Madison this badly terrified her. She wanted to go to her and pull her close again. She wanted to tell her how much she wanted her, how much she longed to take care of her, how much she wanted to be everything to her. But she knew she wouldn't do that, not for real.

She reached under her clothing instead and found her own heat. *She makes me so wet.* She circled her clit and recalled the feel of Madison's kisses, her touch, and the sounds she made. She slipped a finger inside and closed her eyes, and fantasized it was Madison inside of her, taking her to the edge and then pushing her over it. *Oh, god.*

Frustrated enough to cry, she fell asleep asking herself, *Why can't I get out of my own way?*

Sunday

Alex heard a knock on the door adjoining their rooms. She smoothed her freshly showered hair back from her face and pulled it into a ponytail. Madison was already dressed and ready for the day.

"Good morning."

"Hi," Madison said softly.

"Want some coffee? I ordered room service."

"I'd love some." Madison followed her into the room. "How are you feeling?"

You mean besides, I'm falling for you? "Rough," she voiced out loud.

"I guess we got carried away last night, huh?"

"Yeah, I guess we did."

Chapter Seven

Friday

Alex was grateful for a productive workweek, but the same could not be said for her personal life, if you could call it that, where Madison was concerned. They had made small talk in the car during the drive back on Sunday, and Madison had obligations that kept her away from the lab on Monday. Wednesday was so chaotic that they didn't get any downtime to catch up, not to mention time to discuss what had happened the previous weekend. Alex didn't regret what had happened, but she felt ashamed of not being able to express herself properly. She was tongue-tied around Madison on good days with no expectations. How was she going to tell her what she was feeling when it really mattered? Alex shook the thoughts away and walked into the lab. Patricia and team looked up to greet her with smiles all around.

"Good morning, everyone. Give me some good news."

Patricia wasted no time and jumped in. "We had to redo some of the tests when we changed course to try the estrogen receptor, but we're almost done. We are seeing positive results this time with the length of binding time. We have eighty percent of the stability tests ready to show you today and should have the rest to you by the end of next week. If you approve, we can move on to the capability tests right after that."

The team spent the whole morning and the best part of the afternoon together reviewing all the data. Time after time via lapsed videography, Alex watched the modified molecular hybrid, MMH, attach itself to the estrogen receptor on the BRCA mutated gene, forming the BRCA Molecular Modified Gene, or BRCA-MMG. The best part was it stayed there. One hour. Ten hours. Twenty hours. Three days. Five days. It did not relinquish its hold on the gene sequence.

"Excellent work! Nice job everyone. We are so close to checking the box for binding stability." Alex looked at Patricia. "If I approve overtime can you complete the tests earlier? My next read out is at the end of the week, and I need at least a half day to prepare."

"You got it," Patricia said.

"Perfect. Next, who wants to tackle outlining the capability tests for effectively shielding the mutation from attack?" Alex looked around the table. Justin raised two fingers.

"Thanks, Justin."

Alex turned her attention to Tammy. "In our last conversation, you mentioned an interest in becoming more involved with the human clinical trials. Why don't you give some thought to the controls we need in place to measure success with the safety and efficacy in vitro. Let's see if we can make up some time lost in identifying the receptor."

"Okay, yes, I'm very interested. I'll get started right away. Thank you," Tammy said with a pleased expression.

Alex tapped her finger on the table and stood. "I think that's it. Enjoy your weekend."

Alex was tired but in much better spirits when she returned to her office with a little time to spare before her next meeting. Michael arrived a few minutes after her and said hello with a flash of his irresistible smile. Alex responded with her own smile.

"How are the tests going?" Michael asked as he took a seat.

"The team is almost done with the time studies and stability phase. I should have the full data set by next week. I don't want to get ahead of myself, but it's looking good," Alex informed him. "I will keep you posted, and I'll send you the Cliffs Notes version, as I always do."

"Nice, thanks. By the way, David has started the prep work for the next press release, so get ready for the backlash. That's usually the catalyst for an influx of opposition letters. I'll try to shield you from as much flak as I can. I'll have your electronic and physical mail routed to me to preview beginning next week. And just as you have done in the past, try to stay off social media, okay?"

"I'll do my best."

Sensing that Michael seemed uncommonly rushed,

she asked, "Are you all right?"

"It's nothing for you to worry about." Seeing he had not convinced her, he added, "A friend of mine is going through a rough patch, and she has been monopolizing a lot of my free time lately. That's all."

"If you're sure," Alex said.

Michael nodded but Alex wasn't fully convinced.

Saturday

On her way from the barn to the house, Alex looked up when she heard cars enter the driveway. It was Heather and Madison arriving for their morning ride. Alex's heart jumped when Madison smiled and waved.

Alex asked, "Do you guys want some coffee?"

Madison was the first to respond, "Sounds good. I'll help you." Heather left them and walked to the barn.

Standing in the kitchen, Alex studied Madison's appearance. Tan breeches, very complimentary to her figure, paddock boots, and a collared shirt, pristine white, with the top three buttons undone was a good look for her. Barring the riding jacket, she looked more like she was ready for a dressage competition than trail riding. When she realized Madison had caught her staring, she blurted out, "You look amazing."

"I paid attention at the horse show. Did I get everything right?" Madison asked as she looked down at her outfit.

"Yes," was all Alex could say, her tongue tied in knots.

For fuck sake. She needed to figure out a way to reprogram her brain from going into hibernation mode every time Madison showed up, and she needed to do it quickly.

Madison shocked her back to the present when she closed the gap between them and rested her hands at Alex's waist. The contact sent neurons firing fast and furious. The expression on Madison's face was full of questions, but she said, "Are you sure?"

Alex met Madison's gaze and murmured, "Uh huh." *I am now.*

"I've been thinking about last weekend, and I have a lot of questions but right now all I want to do is kiss you again. Is that okay?"

Alex nodded.

The tenderness of Madison's kiss was in sharp contrast to the unyielding countertop behind her as Madison pushed her against it. Madison's lips pressed harder and she responded by parting her own lips, urgently wanting to feel Madison's tongue on hers. She felt Madison's fingers knead her side, sparking a tingling sensation in her midsection. Time seemed to stand still.

"You guys coming?" Heather's voice halted their mini make-out session. Madison reluctantly pulled away. Alex's mind hit the fast-forward button, and her cheeks flushed.

"I guess we better go," Madison said, and they giggled like young girls.

Madison and Alex entered the barn and saw that

Heather had Max already in the cross ties.

Alex said, "Ready to try the grooming?"

"I'm ready," Madison responded.

"Where's your coffee?" Heather asked. Both Madison and Alex looked at each other and giggled again. Heather rolled her eyes at Madison, but she didn't say a word.

After they groomed and tacked up the horses, the three of them headed into the woods. They enjoyed an hour-long ride that included some slow trotting with Alex adding instruction for Madison only when needed. Heather was thrilled to see her friend having such a good time.

After their ride, Madison hung around until Alex had released the horses into the pasture.

"I'd like to make you dinner if you are free next Friday night," Alex said as they walked to Madison's car.

"Oh, I can't do Friday." When she saw the look of disappointment on Alex's face, she quickly added, "Not because I don't want to. I'll be out of town this week on a business trip. I get back late Friday."

"Maybe Saturday evening then?" Alex asked.

"I would like that, Alex."

Wednesday

Midweek, Alex settled on her couch with a glass of wine and her dogs to unwind from her long day. Kenzie and Moose had her flanked on the couch. Kenzie had her head in Alex's lap, and Moose was in the customary four paws up sleeping position. A smile spread across her face when a text from Madison lit up her phone.

"Hi, Alex. How are you?"

"Hi. I'm well. How is your trip going?"

"It's great. Are you busy? Can I call you?"

Madison called a minute later. "I thought it would be easier than texting." There was excitement in her voice as she talked about the seminars she had attended, especially the topics she thought Alex would find interesting.

"Have you gotten all the binding reports yet?" Madison asked, recalling the last lab status.

"Not all of them. Patricia asked for an extension and David's breathing down my neck, but we can't make up the data." Changing the subject, Alex said, "This is such a surprise. I am so glad you called."

"Me too," Madison said, "Lunch today was not the same without you."

"No, it was not." Tossing her filter aside, Alex added, "I'm afraid you have me spoiled already. I was looking forward to another surprise lunch with you." She desperately wanted Madison to know how she made her feel and took advantage of the safety net the phone generated. It seemed easier to form her words when Madison wasn't looking directly at her.

"Well, get used to it. I enjoy spoiling you," Madison flirted. Alex felt the heat rise on her cheeks.

They talked for another half an hour before Madison said, "I should go. Morning comes early." After a short pause she added, "I miss you, Alex."

Alex took a moment to let Madison's heavenly words sink in and then responded, "I miss you too."

Saturday

Alex woke Saturday morning overwhelmed with happiness and anticipation of Madison coming for dinner that night. She jumped out of bed, dressed, and made her way to the barn to enjoy her time with the horses.

The afternoon hours seemed to drag by as Alex waited for Madison, so she busied herself and cleaned the house, finished her laundry, and prepped for dinner. She felt a nervous wave pass through her when she finally heard a car entering the driveway. Alex's nervousness turned to appreciation as she watched Madison walk to the house. Her hair was down, lightly caressing her face. Madison's face lit up when she saw the silent look of approval on Alex's face. They hugged each other in greeting, and as Alex took the bottle of wine from Madison's outstretched hand, she leaned in for a quick kiss.

"Would you care for a glass of wine now?" Alex asked as they entered the kitchen.

"Absolutely!" Madison exclaimed. "Something smells wonderful. What are you making?"

"I'm attempting my sister's chicken piccata recipe, and I hope I do it justice," Alex said. "It's almost ready. How about a tour since you've really only seen the kitchen so far?"

Madison responded, "Yes, and since I already know I really like your kitchen, I cannot wait to see what the rest of the house feels like."

Alex's insides did a now familiar somersault when Madison's teasing eyes met hers. Alex seemed to be at the mercy of her body's response when Madison teased her, and it didn't matter whether it was a teasing look or tone of her voice. It made her feel alive. Alex reached for Madison's hand, and they stayed close as they walked through the living room, laundry, and mudroom. They climbed the stairs to tour the rooms on the second floor. When they got to Alex's bedroom, Madison stepped inside and took a complete circle around the room. All of Alex's nerves stood at full attention. *She's standing in my bedroom.* Seeing Madison standing there, in her private space, elicited an almost primal response. On those occasions when she did go home with someone, she always let them take her to their place. She had shared this room with no one.

The kitchen timer beeped. "Are you hungry?" Alex asked.

Madison answered, "I'm starving." A grin played on her lips. They made their way back downstairs.

Alex picked up her phone and asked, "What kind of music do you like?"

"I like all kinds. Depends on my mood."

"And what would your mood like to listen to at the moment?" Alex teased back, liking how easy it was to do.

"I think some soft rock will do."

"Soft rock it is."

"What can I do?" Madison asked.

"Sit and enjoy your wine." Madison was about to protest, but Alex stopped her. "It's my turn to treat you."

Madison chose a bar stool at the island. She watched Alex rinse angel hair pasta before pouring it into the pan with the simmering chicken. Alex added the remaining herbs and more lemon with deliberation. When the last timer went off, she took a tray of sliced Italian bread smothered with olive oil and garlic from the oven and pulled a bowl of salad from the refrigerator. She arranged the pasta, bread, and salad on the island in her typical organized fashion.

"Oh, that looks and smells so good."

Alex took a quick sip of her wine and said, "Let's eat."

Conversation flowed easily as they talked about their week and listened to the music Madison had chosen for them. After dinner, they took turns picking songs to listen to and Alex opened a second bottle of wine after they moved to the couch.

"So where will your next vacation take you?" Alex asked.

"Well, let's see. London and Greece are on my short list. I haven't been to either place yet. How about you?"

"I've been to London but not Greece," Alex said.

"Tell me about London. What did you see and do there?"

Alex always enjoyed talking about places she had visited. She especially enjoyed telling Madison about the trip she and Callie had taken to England. Alex told her about arriving at Heathrow Airport and staying in a hotel near Trafalgar Square. She and Callie toured the Tower of London, where they had afternoon tea and viewed the Crown Jewels, and they visited Westminster Abbey, Kensington Palace, and Buckingham Palace. They watched the Queen's Changing of the Guard and walked through the Queen's stables where they learned that the Queen personally named every horse stabled there. The stable area was also home to all the beautiful, lavish horse-drawn carriages.

"It sounds like an amazing trip," Madison said. "I would love to see Kensington Palace and Buckingham Palace and Westminster Abbey. Thinking about walking through the abbey, surrounded by all that history, gives me goosebumps."

After a few moments of quiet reflection, Madison jumped from her seat and said, "I love this song. Dance with me."

"Really?" Alex asked.

"Well, I do owe you a dance," Madison answered and pulled Alex to her feet. She smiled, acknowledging how their evening at the bar had ended.

Madison held Alex close. Madison found rhythm with the music, and Alex simply allowed herself to follow her lead. Madison's hands traveled up and down Alex's arms, around her waist, and across her lower back. Her touch accelerated the already intoxicating effects of the wine. Madison's gaze never wavered from Alex's as they shared each other's personal space through the rest of one song and into the next.

"What are you thinking?" Madison asked.

Before she lost her nerve, Alex said, "I'm thinking I want to get lost in you, and it scares me."

"I can relate." Not wanting to ruin the mood but taking the gamble anyway, Madison asked, "Can you tell me what happened the weekend of the horse show?" Alex's body stiffened, but she didn't move away. Alex pulled Madison toward the couch with her. Alex chose her words carefully.

"Madison, I told you I didn't want to be more than friends because I struggle to let people in, to allow myself to feel, or to open up the way a relationship like that requires. I haven't been able to hang on to the special people I've cared for that deeply," Alex said, her eyes bright with tears.

Madison's tone was soothing, "Slow down, Alex. Are you talking about your dad?"

"And Kate."

Appreciating how hard Alex was trying, Madison softly said, "Alex, it's okay. You don't have to tell me."

"No. I want to tell you. Losing my dad messed me up, no news flash there." Alex looked at Madison with a shaky grin, trying to add some levity to keep herself talking. "It took me a long time before I was ready to try being in a relationship that required more than sex, but Kate made it easy. She was kind and patient. Things between us were going great, and we moved in together. And then I was offered an amazing opportunity to lead a DNA mapping project, which Kate totally supported. It required me to be away for longer and longer periods of time and that took its toll. When she needed more from me, I wasn't there for her." Alex dropped her head. "I hurt her." Alex made eye contact with Madison. "I don't want to hurt you like that."

"Then don't."

Alex sighed and some of the earlier tension released. Talking like this felt good. It gave her hope that maybe, just maybe, there was a chance that her story with Madison could be different.

"Alex, I'm not Kate and knowing what you know now, you can make different choices. No one is forcing you to make the same decisions you made in the past."

Alex smiled and ran her finger down Madison's cheek and cradled her chin with her thumb. "Do you know how amazing you are? Where have you been all this time?"

"I think maybe waiting for you."

Madison pulled Alex into her arms and whispered into her hair, "Besides, I've developed quite a weakness for you, so I'm not planning on going anywhere." She leaned into Alex to seal her promise with a soft kiss.

Sunday

Alex woke Sunday morning feeling a need for intervention, and in only the way Callie could provide it. Madison consumed her thoughts and she needed advice. She battled with her inner psyche that always tried to play it safe. Alex planned and prepared for everything. After her dad died, her plan was to focus on school, get her degree, and make something of herself. She allowed no place for relationships, at least not long-term ones that had the potential to put her plan at risk. Loving people and losing people were distractions, an interference.

Kate had thrown a wrench into her plan when she made Alex feel things she had not felt before. Self-doubt chipped away at her armor and the importance she had placed solely on her work and her career. Kate told her that her work was important but that it wasn't what was most important in her life. She told her that the people she surrounded herself with and the relationships built with those people were the ultimate gifts in life.

Alex had struggled to find a way to balance her work and her relationship with Kate. She had wanted to make Kate a priority in her life, but every time she had an opportunity to do so, she allowed her research to pull her in the opposite direction. She was always busy or working on something groundbreaking that needed her attention. Her research consumed her to the extent that she could not even pinpoint when Kate started to pull away and become distant. In fact, she was unaware until the day Kate left.

Playing it from the safety of the sidelines had backfired on her. She didn't want too little too late again. Though she usually allowed herself to be pulled away from anyone who distracted her from her research, Alex found she did not want that to happen with Madison.

Callie arrived at Alex's house in the afternoon with pizza and beer. She let herself in, calling out her arrival as she closed the door. Moose and Kenzie greeted her with excited whimpers and lots of tail wagging.

Alex gave her friend a tight hug. "Thanks for coming."

They got themselves set up in the living room, putting their food and drink on the coffee table before Callie asked, "What's going on?"

"I'm in trouble."

Callie put her beer down. "What happened? Did someone threaten you? I knew it. Ever since that night you and Michael came to the bar downplaying any threats, I've had a bad feeling."

"No, no, it's not that. At least, not that I'm aware of." Alex paused. "It's Madison."

"Go on."

Alex gave a detailed recap of her time spent with Madison from their weekend at the horse show to their last serious conversation.

"Having dinner at her place was like taking a step back in time to when Amber and I were young, spending family time together during the holidays. Her place is inviting, and she's warm and caring and attentive. She has a way of pulling me in and making me feel comfortable. Time seems to slow down when I'm with her. I'm totally consumed by thoughts of her. And her body, Callie, her body is amazing. Her touch invokes an incredible response from mine, one like I've never felt before, and my brain implodes every time a make-out session could lead to sex, and I bail because I'm afraid of losing control with her. She feels like all the good things about home, all wrapped into one, and it scares the living shit out of me."

"Home," Callie repeated.

Callie searched Alex's face for further confirmation,

and reveled in the moment, before she said, "Fuck, Alex. She sounds amazing and you, my friend, are falling for her, really hard." She put her hand over her opened mouth and stared at Alex.

"But what do I do now?"

"What do you want to do?"

Frustrated when Callie's response to her question was another question, she exclaimed, "I don't know because my brain doesn't function properly when I'm around her!"

"Does she feel the same way?"

"She hasn't said it exactly, but I think so."

Callie laughed at the pained expression on Alex's face. "All the complicated science thingamajigs you solve and you struggle with this." Callie grabbed Alex's arm and tugged on it. "If she's as amazing as she sounds, she'll be willing to work through this stuff with you. Talk to her already and find out, would you?"

Alex threw a pillow at her with an exasperated sigh.

"Your turn. What's been going on with Tina?"

"I asked her to dinner the night after she disappeared on me, and she accepted. We went back to my place afterward for a really amazing make-out session on my couch. She was more than willing, but something made me put the brakes on."

"I'm sorry, what?" asked Alex, with a dumbfounded expression on her face.

"I stopped us." Callie shook her head, "I don't know, I just felt like I needed her to slow down."

"Oh my god, you're serious, *you* bailed? The queen of love 'em and leave 'em?"

"I know, but there is something mysterious about her that I like. She's a little quiet and withdrawn, and she doesn't open up easily nor, I would guess, trust easily. She didn't have the best childhood, and her family alienated her when she came out, so not surprisingly, she sees a counselor regularly. She makes me want to take my time with her and draw it out. She may be a tough nut to crack, but one I think I'm going to enjoy." Callie smiled sheepishly.

Alex's protective side kicked in, and she said, "Be careful, Callie. You know what they say about the quiet ones."

"What? That they're good in bed?"

"How would you know since you haven't slept with her yet?" Alex teased.

Callie grunted and threw the pillow back at her, "Touché."

Chapter *Eight*

Saturday

The next weekend, Alex woke to an overcast and unseasonably chilly Saturday morning with an anxious but not unpleasant feeling in her gut. Madison had been coming to ride for so many weekends at this point, it was hard for Alex to remember what it was like not having her here. She fit into her special place so well that Alex's thoughts wandered to what it would be like to have her here more than just on Saturdays. Alex was tidying up around the barn when she heard Madison's car in the driveway.

Alex's attraction to Madison was undeniable and becoming more and more intense. Madison pulled Alex against her and gave her a tight squeeze before she pulled away to kiss her tenderly. The warmth in her kiss spread through Alex's body, down the length of her arms and legs, leaving her feeling all gooey. They stood there wrapped in each other's arms for several seconds.

Alex finally broke the silence. "Is Heather coming today?"

"No, she isn't feeling well."

"Just us then," said Alex. She took Madison's hand in hers as they made their way to the horses.

Dark clouds hovered in the sky above them. A loose chain clanked against one of the metal gates in the wind, and Alex pulled her collar closer around her neck. She hoped they would have enough time for a short trail ride before the rain came.

Madison shivered as they walked to the barn. Alex led her to a small cabinet in the bathroom where she kept heavier riding clothing. She handed Madison a long sleeve top and turned to leave to give Madison privacy, but when she moved to close the door, she was caught off guard by the sight of bare skin. Madison's back was toward her and exposed except for her sports bra as she pulled off her top and replaced it with the heavier one Alex had given her. Alex commanded her eyes to look away, but they would not obey. They stayed glued to Madison's tan figure. Her pulse quickened and her stomach tightened as she remembered how smooth her skin felt under her touch.

"I'm ready," Madison said as she walked out of the small room and joined Alex by the stalls.

Alex had to clear her throat before she could respond. She busied herself with Dunkin's halter and slipped it over his head.

They rode in a peaceful silence with Alex frequently

looking over at Madison to see how she was doing. Madison wore a contented smile on her face. Alex felt a pleasant sensation course through her when she realized there was more to having Madison physically here, sharing this special time and place with her. Madison gave this place even more meaning. Alex had not thought that was possible. Would Madison be willing to work on figuring out where these feelings would take them together? *I won't know until I ask*, Alex thought. Madison had been outright about her feelings of attraction toward her, and there was an undeniable pull between them. Alex just had to figure out a way to shut off that voice telling her she would never be able to give enough. *Ask, out loud.*

"I was talking to Callie, and she thinks you might be good for me," Alex said as she watched Madison's face to gauge her reaction.

"Oh, yeah? Your friend is a good judge of character. I haven't met her yet, but I like her already."

The sound of Madison's laughter sent another jolt through Alex. She wanted to pull Madison into her arms and never let her go. A light mist began to fall around them.

Summoning the courage, Alex said, "I'm good at closing myself off." Her voice got softer as she added, "But I don't want to do that with you."

Madison said, "Hey, look at me." The horses had come to a stop side by side. Alex slowly reconnected her gaze with Madison's. Her pulse was pounding in her ears. "I don't want you to either."

Madison's eyes were so very blue. She wanted to swim

in those oceans forever. The mist turned into a steady rain, and they turned the horses around. The rain showered both horses and riders. No tack or clothing was left dry by the time they made it back to the barn. They quickly untacked the horses and got them settled in their stalls.

Alex said, "Come up to the house to dry off."

Madison smoothed her hair back from her face and looked down at her wet clothes and said, "Good idea."

Madison watched Alex as she held the door open for her. Her black hair was tousled by the wind and rain and her long sleeve t-shirt clung to her tall frame. Madison's resolve to give Alex the time she needed waned as she watched Alex begin to undress in front of her as they moved into the mud room. Alex stripped out of her dripping jacket and boots. She picked up a couple clean towels from the top of the dryer and handed one to Madison. She absent-mindedly pulled her wet tee-shirt over her head and threw it in the washing machine. She started unbuttoning her breeches and stopped only to run the towel over her hair to catch the drops of rain gathering at the ends. The crest of her underwear was visible just under a sliver of the sleek skin of her abdomen.

Madison heard herself let out an involuntary sound but tried to mask her reaction, and said jokingly, "Is there any look you can't pull off?"

Alex pulled the towel from her head and saw Madison staring at her. Alex followed her gaze and looked down. Her white tank top was soaked through and her nipples were hard and pressed against the fabric. A wave of embarrassment washed over her, and she instinctively tried to pull the material away from her body. The movement just intensified the heat in Madison's gaze. She was standing a few feet away and yet Alex felt the burn as if she had been a scorched log ablaze in a fireplace.

"Do you know how sexy you look right now?"

Alex simply stood there staring at her. She was the eye of the storm, with her mind running in circles, so many thoughts swirling around her with a fury. But she found herself surprisingly calm. The realization occurred to her that she knew exactly what she wanted. She was looking at exactly what she wanted.

"Fuck," Madison exhaled through a short breath.

Madison moved toward her with a force Alex couldn't stop, didn't want to stop, she admitted to herself. Alex didn't want to brace herself against this storm. She wanted to welcome her in, swallow her whole, worship her. Physically wanting this woman took a back seat to something deeper. She wanted to know every intimate inch of her, achingly so, but she wanted her in her world, sharing her space, sharing her life with her, and the feelings overwhelmed her.

With huskiness in her voice, Madison said, "Alex, I . . ."

The desire in Madison's eyes was piercing, and Alex felt all the hair on her body stand at attention. Madison's lips found hers, and it was the match that lit the fire low in her belly. She felt her own desire steady her and overshadow the voice that always told her to run.

She parted her lips and immediately felt Madison's tongue searching for hers. Alex didn't hesitate, and greeted her, stroke for stroke as their tongues danced together. Alex's invitation to deepen their kiss by tugging and sucking on her tongue was met with a soft groan from Madison. She yielded and eased her body into Madison's. The chill from the cold rain just moments ago turned into a raging fire enveloping her skin. Time stood still, her mind shrouded in a fog. The pounding of her heart sounded in her ears as their kisses became more urgent and demanding. Madison pushed her body harder against Alex and ran her hands from Alex's waist to the small of her back to pull her impossibly closer.

Madison, attempting one last ditch effort to regain a thread of composure, asked, "Are you sure?"

"Yes," said Alex. Her statement made Madison shiver.

"Are you cold?" Alex asked, without moving away, reminded that they were still in wet clothes. Madison looked at her with a smoldering look that matched her own and answered her question completely. Overwhelmed with desire, Alex whispered against Madison's lips, "Come with me." She led Madison through the house and up the stairs.

She pulled Madison with her into the shower. The hot water and steam accelerated the heat between them. Alex struggled to catch her breath. They hastily removed what remained of their wet clothing and began exploring each other's naked bodies frantically with their hands and mouths.

"Alex, touch me, please."

Alex did as Madison asked, and she heard Madison moan as she slid her hand between Madison's legs and found her hot, wet folds. The circles she traced through her heat were deliberate with one purpose in mind.

"Oh god," Madison gasped.

Alex pulled herself away just enough to make eye contact with those dark stormy oceans of blue. With that one look, Alex, coming completely unhinged, brimmed with confidence. Feeling an overwhelming desire to do or give Madison anything she wanted, a seductively mischievous smile formed on her lips as she asked, "What else do you want?"

Without hesitation, Madison pleaded, "I want to feel you inside of me when you make me come." Alex wrapped her arm around Madison to hold her close as she slipped inside of her. Alex let out a groan of her own as Madison clenched around her fingers. Madison grabbed Alex's shoulders to steady herself and her body bucked and shuttered against Alex as she climaxed. Her legs were like jelly, boneless, and she silently thanked the supportive arm wrapped around her, holding her up.

Madison's eyes still smoldered when she reclaimed Alex's mouth feverishly and took command of Alex's body with an equal measure of desire. With their need for each other not yet satisfied, Madison whispered in Alex's ear, "Take me to bed."

Bodies barely dry, Alex stopped in front of Madison by the edge of the bed. Alex stood there and stared at her like a moth seeking its flame. She paused. She was suddenly caught up in the fact that Madison was now standing, totally naked, in her bedroom. This shouldn't surprise her though, should it? Ever since approaching her at the bar that night, Madison had been breaking all her rules, hadn't she? She showed up in her office, then at the barn, her place of solitude, and now here in her most intimate space.

Madison sensed her hesitation and placing a hand on Alex's forearm asked, "What is it?"

"This is just overwhelming me right now."

"We don't have to—"

"No, it's not—it's a good thing. I want this," Alex placed her hand over Madison's. "It's just, I've never had anyone here with me before."

Madison's expression was first one of confusion and then understanding. She put on a sly grin and said, "So, I'm your first, huh?"

An adorably shy smile spread across Alex's face. A warm sensation washed over Madison, and if she could have melted right there on the spot, she would have. Alex cupped Madison's face as she placed a teasing kiss on her lips and then kissed her down the side of her neck and across her shoulder. Her eyes raked up and down Madison's body and when their eyes met, her desire to satisfy Madison's needs came flooding back.

"I so want to take my time with you, getting to know every inch of your beautiful body."

"Well, I don't have anywhere I have to be today," Madison whispered.

"But first . . ." Alex's gaze dropped to Madison's mouth when her lips parted to draw in a breath.

Alex stepped closer and when Madison made no motion to resist, she cupped Madison's breast and thumbed her nipple. She lowered her head and pulled the hard peak into her mouth and sucked on it. Madison gasped. Alex ran her hands over Madison's stomach and hips and down the front of her thighs as she knelt in front of her. She closed her eyes and paused to savor the scent of Madison's arousal before running her hands up the back of her legs and cupping her bottom to pull her closer. She ran the flat of her tongue over Madison's swollen mound as she slid her fingers through her wet folds and drove them deep inside of her.

"Down. Bed. Now," Madison gasped.

Alex stood without breaking their connection and pushed Madison onto the bed and covered her with her body. She reclaimed Madison's mouth with a deep hunger before moving lower. The feel of Madison's body and her response to Alex's touch was bringing Alex to the brink of her own climax.

"Oh god, I'm going to come again," Madison cried out. Alex stilled to enjoy her orgasm as she came in her mouth.

"Holy shit, Alex." Madison inhaled deeply to slow her breathing.

"I want to do that again," Alex said.

Madison stopped her. She pulled Alex up and rolled over to straddle her. "Who says you get to have all the fun?" Madison smiled at Alex, full on dimples, and Alex felt her stomach tighten in anticipation.

Monday

Monday morning rolled around again, way too quickly, and Trevor's voice carried into Alex's office. "Sure, Madison, let me get her for you. One moment please."

Alex paused a moment and took a deep breath before answering, "Good morning, Madison."

"Hi, Alex. Good morning. I know you are busy, so I don't want to keep you. I just wanted you to know that I was thinking about you, and I enjoyed our time together Saturday."

Alex responded, "I did too." She wanted to say more, but she stopped herself. This was not the place to share what she was thinking right now.

"Good, then I'll see you Wednesday for lunch?" Madison asked.

"Yes, I can't wait to see you." Alex disconnected the call and turned her focus to the task at hand but found it increasingly difficult to resist daydreams of a naked Madison in her bedroom.

Wednesday

Wednesday morning staff meeting always began with team updates. Everyone was seated around the conference room table. Alex was physically sitting in her conference room chair, but her mind was running away with her. She stood in her shower and she ran a hand down over Madison's stomach and between her legs. She heard Madison moan.

"Alex?" Patricia had to repeat herself before she got Alex's attention.

Shaking her head and snapping her gaze to the tabletop image, Alex responded, "I'm sorry, Patricia. What were you saying?"

"We are finished. The results are conclusive. The BRCA-MMG passed the last of the binding stability tests this morning. It's working."

Patricia's words rushed into Alex's brain. "It's working . . . it's working!" she repeated to herself.

"We did it, Alex, we did it!" Patricia all but shouted.

Alex's thoughts were in sudden turmoil. Even with Patricia's monumental declaration, Alex found her thoughts returning to Madison. She wished Madison was here to share the moment. Criticizing herself for not having more self-control to keep distractions at bay, she let the swirl of emotions compete for a moment before regaining focus and allowing herself to speak again.

"Show me. I want to see it again." Alex had imagined this moment for such a long time. She had to be sure.

Patricia understood and started typing on the table's invisible keyboard. An image began to appear. There it was. The BRCA Molecular Modified Gene, BRCA-MMG, remained intact within the cell.

"Holy shit!" Alex heard herself exclaim. She let the gravity of the situation sink in for everyone for a moment before she said, "Okay, let's review the rest of the analysis. Take me through it step by step."

The team spent several hours reviewing each step

of the study with Alex to ensure nothing critical was missed. They examined all the biological markers they had tried, reviewed the stability test results for each, and the length of binding times. They recorded the results of the BRCA-MMG under different temperature and medium conditions.

Once they had exhausted protocol, Patricia concluded with, "I think we are ready to introduce the next phase and test the new molecular entity's capability of shielding the mutated gene against attack. I will re-direct a sub team to begin developing the test scenarios Justin has outlined."

Alex nodded. Reflecting for a moment, she said, "Consolidate the binding reports for me by this time tomorrow. I cannot thank you guys enough for the tremendous work you have done here. You are all a part of history in the making. Time for me to head upstairs to share the news."

Before Alex left the room, Patricia called after her, "Meet at the restaurant on Friday, right?"

Alex paused and turned around to see her team looking at her with puzzled expressions at what she could only assume was a response to her somewhat peculiar behavior.

"Of course we will," and attempting to sound more like her normal self, she added, "Let's meet at seven."

On her way to David's office, she stopped at the restroom to splash cold water on her face. She stared at her reflection, and her thoughts wandered again. This was *the* day she had been working so hard for. She had planned and prepared for this day for a long time. Alex was not a stranger to enjoying milestones when it came to the progress of her research, but this one was different. This was a major milestone that could open the door to so much more to come. This could possibly beat breast cancer. The next phase of the research would begin to validate their theories. This was what Alex had been groomed for and here she was distracted by her thoughts of Madison.

Why is this happening now? Alex thought as she stared at herself in the mirror. "Get your head back in the game, Alex," she said as she squared her shoulders.

Alex updated David and Michael on the news and received approval to begin the next phase as planned. The next several weeks would involve capability test strategy sessions, running the test scenarios in the lab, and consolidating the successful binding stability data into a single report for the FDA. This meant combing through hundreds of pages of data and organizing it in such a way to enable federal auditors to follow and understand each and every step she and her team had performed in the lab, along with the required statistical results from each test performed.

Madison called around noon to confirm their lunch date, and Alex shared the news with her.

"I am thrilled for you, Alex. Congratulations!" Madison shouted through the phone.

"Thank you, Madison. I don't think it has really sunk in yet. We have a lot of work ahead of us, and we need to get started right away. I may be out of pocket for a couple weeks. I'm sorry." Despite the sense of uneasiness that washed over her even as the words left her mouth, she added nothing more.

"Don't apologize, Alex. I get it. Go do what you do."

"Thank you for understanding, Madison. Can you make dinner with the team this Friday?"

"Oh, Sutton, Derek, and I are getting together for dinner at my parent's house on Friday. I could try to get out of it."

"No, don't cancel. Spend the time with your family."

"Are you sure?" asked Madison.

"Absolutely." So why did it suddenly feel like there was an elephant sitting on her chest?

Friday

The team was loud and boisterous throughout dinner, and the waitress was kept busy with her frequent trips back and forth to the bar ensuring no one ran out of their favorite beverage. Even though the dinner was technically meant to celebrate their recent milestone, the team was excited and spent most of the evening planning their next phase. Halfway through dinner, to everyone's surprise, David and Michael walked up to their table.

"I just wanted everyone to know what an amazing job you have done, and I wanted to personally thank you and toast each and every one of you," David said and raised his glass. "Here's to all of you. Without your hard work, dedication, and perseverance, we would not be here tonight. Thank you." Though not the norm to hear kind words from David, his words sounded heartfelt, and the team welcomed both men to their celebration.

After dinner, Michael walked Alex to her car. "So how about a nightcap at my place?" Michael asked, his words slightly slurred. She turned to face him before opening her car door.

"Michael, I can't." Alex added, "I've met someone."

"So? That doesn't mean we can't celebrate, does it? I mean, we are so good at it." Michael pushed Alex up against her car and before she could raise her hands to intercept him, he kissed her.

"Michael, no." Alex pushed him away, but did so gently. "Hey," she waited for him to look at her. "We never hooked up when you were with someone." Alex searched his face and waited for a look of recognition and acceptance. Michael reluctantly backed away and hung his head.

"Okay, see you Monday." He walked toward his car.

Alex got in her car and pulled out of the parking lot, unaware that Madison had been waiting there to surprise her.

Madison watched in shock as Michael pushed Alex up against her car and kissed her. She could not hear what was said, but they seemed incredibly familiar with each other. She had been so excited to surprise Alex on her special night that she had left her parent's house right after dinner. But now she chastised herself for getting too carried away with Alex, knowing full well she wasn't ready for anything serious. She sat in stunned silence and watched Michael get into his car and follow Alex out of the parking lot.

Chapter *Nine*

Wednesday

"What do you think?" Michael was looking out the window, his arms crossed over his chest. The morning fog clung to the surrounding buildings like a bride's veil.

Behind the scenes, Michael had been discreetly acting as gatekeeper to Alex's emails and social media feeds for weeks, monitoring for anything suspicious, threatening, or harmful. It began with a seemingly nondescript subject line that read "research" sent via company emails and addressed to Alex's inbox. The message explained why the sender didn't agree with the direction of Alex's research and went on to say that the research should stop immediately. No outright threat yet. But Michael's experience put him on high alert. Events such as these usually started small and seemed insignificant but then occasionally and without warning, they would ignite a slow burn that could quickly get out of control. His gut told him to stay ahead of this one.

Not long after the initial email, several more were received and included stronger language on views in opposition to the company's direction and became more pointedly directed at Alex as the ringmaster. This morning Michael was greeted by a delivery messenger with a legal sized, manila envelope addressed to Alex. The messenger was reluctant to release the package to Michael, telling him that he had specific instructions to deliver it to Alex in person, but when Michael told the young man that seeing Alex wasn't going to happen, he didn't push back and seemed just as satisfied with getting on with the rest of his day.

The emails had prompted Michael to keep a closer eye out for Alex and her team, but the package was the catalyst for him to take further action and to do so meant he had to engage David.

"I don't like it," said David, "but I don't want you to tell Alex. This will only rattle her, and I need her focused right now. We can't afford any more delays." David scanned the pictures strewn over his desk again. The manila envelope contained various photos of Alex, a shot of her in her car pulling out of the company's parking garage, Alex leaving a bar, and Alex sitting at a table in a restaurant having dinner.

"I have to tell her something, David. At least grant me permission to assign a protective detail to her if it comes to that."

"Fine. But no details, you hear me? We have too much riding on this."

Michael wanted to push back but reluctantly agreed instead.

Alex finished up her morning routine and skimmed her schedule for the rest of the day. She saw that Trevor had booked Michael over her lunchtime hour. Her hour with Madison. She felt a twinge of frustration and then disappointment.

"Trevor," she yelled from her seat. Assessing her tone, Trevor rushed into her office.

"What does Michael need that cannot wait until this afternoon?"

"He wasn't specific, he just said he had to see you."

"Okay."

Trevor retreated from the room. He could see Alex was frustrated, and he thought he could guess why. She had been acting so differently since Madison had started consulting with them.

Alex physically shook herself as if to shake loose her feeling of disappointment. She reached for her phone to text Madison about the change of plans.

Michael arrived early and seemed agitated when he walked into the office. He didn't usually lose his cool.

"Hey, what's going on? Trevor said you needed to see me and that it couldn't wait until our normal time this afternoon."

"I need to talk to you, Alex. Let's go out for lunch."

Thrown off by his unusual behavior, Alex simply agreed and stood up to follow him.

Once they placed their order at the corner diner, Alex said, "Michael, you are freaking me out. What's going on?"

Michael said, "I wanted to apologize for my behavior Friday night." Alex put her hand up to stop him.

"It's fine. Don't worry about it." Sensing there was more to this impromptu meeting she added, "What's happened?"

"I struggled with whether or not to share this with you, and I don't mean to scare you."

"What?"

"The office has been getting threatening emails since the press release."

"That's nothing unusual. Lots of people voice their opinions when we release updates."

"There have also been emails to your account threatening you specifically."

"What do they say?"

"I don't want you to get caught up in this. You'll only worry about it."

"Well, you told me now. I can't just go back to not knowing," Alex said, raising her voice.

"I told you so you would be extra careful." Michael reached across the table to take Alex's hand in hopes of calming her down.

"How do I do that?"

"I've asked one of my cop friends to keep an eye on the office, you, and your team. So, if you see a big guy hanging around, he's just here as a precaution, okay?"

"You think someone may try to hurt one of us?"

Michael reluctantly added, "The emails suggest bodily harm if your research isn't stopped." Michael watched Alex processing the information.

"What should we do?"

"Just keep doing what you are doing. I'm in close contact with my local precinct buddies, and I've hired a private investigator to help out. On top of being a great PI, he's also tech savvy. I have no doubt he'll be able to pin down the location of the IP address in no time." Michael looked tired.

"Okay," Alex said. "How is your friend?"

Michael grimaced. "She's struggling with mental illness, and I feel a family obligation to help her. It's a little taxing." He looked at this watch noting their hour was about up. "Long story, maybe another time?"

Alex didn't press.

Friday

As Alex pulled into her driveway after a grueling five day stretch of planning and creating new test scenarios, she saw Madison's car parked there. She felt her weariness fade. Her mood lifted when she saw Madison sitting on the porch step.

"Aren't you a sight for sore eyes." *I've missed you*, she thought.

"I hope this is okay, just showing up like this. I just wanted to see you. We seem to be moving in different circles the last couple weeks."

"Of course it's okay, and yeah, it's been so busy with getting all the data compiled for the final report, I hardly even know what day it is."

Alex stopped in front of Madison. Under the porch lighting, Madison saw dark circles under Alex's eyes. Madison reached out for Alex wanting to comfort her but stopped herself. Alex noticed her withdraw.

"What's going on?" Alex searched her face but found no answer. "Come inside," Alex said as she walked into the house to put her things down. Madison followed her into the kitchen.

Alex instinctively fell back on one of her old habits of filling the silence with excuses, which generated an unwelcome déjà vu. "I'm sorry I haven't been engaged lately. I get distracted with work and lose all sense of time."

Madison hesitated as if she was trying to find the right words, "I understand you getting caught up with work. I get that," she paused, "what I don't understand is what I saw the other night and I . . ." Madison's voice caught in her throat. She looked at Alex with a confused, disappointed look on her face.

"The other night? What are you talking about?"

"That night at the restaurant. I saw you, Alex. I saw you kissing Michael."

"You were at the restaurant? Why didn't you tell me?"

"I wanted to surprise you, but I didn't want to interrupt your celebration with your team, so I waited outside. Then I saw you and Michael kissing, and I left." Madison took a deep breath, "Alex, I've asked you this before, and

I'm going to ask you again, am I misreading us and this, whatever this is, that's happening between us?" Madison's attempts to stop the tears failed, and Alex moved closer to console her, but Madison pulled back to avoid her touch.

"Madison, it's not what it looked like."

"Oh my god, don't say that. It was exactly what it looked like."

"What I mean is, you did not see *us* kissing. He kissed me, and I pushed him away, and we both went home alone. Nothing happened, and there is nothing between us."

"Jesus Christ. You told me you weren't dating him." She gasped as the realization hit her, "You're just fucking him. Got it." Madison took another step backwards to steady herself against the countertop.

"We saw each other casually—before us," Alex admitted.

"Us. Right," Madison said, shaking her head. "I'm not used to feeling jealous, but when I saw him touching you, I don't know what happened. I just know I didn't like it." Their eyes connected, and the hurt residing there pierced Alex's soul.

"Madison, I do not have romantic feelings for him. In fact, I cannot think about anything else but you. You consume my thoughts all the time. I go to bed thinking about you, and I wake up thinking about you. Honestly, I think about you throughout most of the day. Even when I am trying to work, I find myself daydreaming about you and the time we've spent together."

"Then why do I still feel like you verbalize one thing and your actions show another? You told me you want to open up with me, but your actions create a distance between us. Do you even realize how long it's been since you've called or texted me?"

Alex dropped her head. "Please believe me when I say that I honestly want this to work with us, but my work—people's lives are on the line."

"I know your work is important, Alex, but what about you?"

"I've dedicated my life to my research. This is who I am." And there it was. That déjà vu feeling was back.

"Your work is what you do, and yes, it's important, and yes, it's a part of your life story, but it is not who you are. The true gifts in life are the people we love and the people who love us in return. They give us our true purpose in life and make us who we are."

"My work can give many people better, longer lives."

"By sacrificing your own happiness and fulfillment, Alex? That doesn't seem fair."

Alex fidgeted and not knowing how to respond, she remained quiet. She desperately wanted Madison to understand her, but she was conflicted, and she was beginning to doubt the things she had always told herself. Madison made her believe there was more to life than she currently allowed herself to have. Alex realized that she wanted Madison to be part of that alternate future if it really existed for her. She just didn't know how to get there from here. The air around them was heavy and after a long silence, Madison stood up to leave.

"Madison, please don't go."

Madison winced when she heard the pleading in Alex's voice, but she stood her ground, "Alex, I should have listened to the repeated signs telling me you weren't ready, but I ignored them because as hard as I try not to, I'm falling for you." Her voice cracked as her tears started to fall.

Alex felt all the air escape from her lungs.

Madison started toward the door and turned around one more time. "I can't do this, Alex. It's my fault for pushing you into something you aren't ready for. I will give you the space you can't seem to ask for yourself."

Alex could do nothing but watch her leave and that tightness in her chest clamped down like a vise-grip.

Chapter *Ten*

Saturday

Alex woke the next morning on the couch, alone. Even the dogs seemed to sense she was conflicted and were leery of her. She had to coax them to her by putting on a pretense before they returned to their usual playful selves. The evening before came rushing back to her. Madison. She looked out the front window hoping to see a familiar car, but it was not there. She felt nauseous. She decided on a shower, hoping it would make her feel better and hoping Madison would show up eventually. She never did.

Friday

Madison kept to her word about giving Alex space. Three more weeks passed without a word from or sight of Madison. She stopped bringing lunch, and she stopped joining Alex on Saturday for horseback riding. She even ended her consulting contract with the lab.

Alex wanted to talk to Madison, but she was still at a loss for words to explain what she wanted, so she did the only thing she knew how to do. She dove into her work, trying harder than ever to concentrate. By the fourth week, the team had reached yet another milestone when the outcomes of the capability tests were successful. The molecule protected the mutated gene from every attack scenario they tested. The final pre-trial hurdle was passed and all the clinical scenarios for the first human trial were prepared. Alex's team received FDA approval to test their new medication, Bregensaf, in human subjects in a Phase 1 Clinical Trial.

Several life-science companies were engaged through the grant sponsors to bid on funding and on manufacturing the medication for the clinical trial. The local and national news authorities were contacted to prepare for a press release. The excitement in the lab was almost tangible.

They held their customary celebration dinner, and Alex had hoped that by some small stroke of luck Madison would try to surprise her again, but she didn't show. She thought about going home with Michael but knew he wouldn't be able to satisfy her. Even with all the project's success, one thing was certain, something had changed. Alex had changed and whatever it was, it was not letting her go. Alex excused herself earlier than usual. Trevor and Patricia looked at each other in concern as they watched her leave.

Alex made her way straight to Callie's bar and slumped in the seat of their favorite booth. She drew in a long breath and then slowly let it escape. Callie swooped in with two glasses and an opened bottle of red wine in tow.

"Spill it, let's hear it."

"Where to start?" Alex searched Callie's face as if she'd find the answer there and took a sip of her wine.

Alex started rambling. "Madison is absolutely amazing. Perfect, really. We have a great time talking, listening to music, and dancing. She's funny, clever, intellectual, and traveled. She is close with her family, and she's available. Her last serious relationship ended years ago." Alex paused to take another sip of her wine. "And the sex is mind blowing, like an orgasm on steroids."

Callie raised her eyebrows, "So you were able to shut down the flight response, huh?"

Alex nodded.

Sensing Alex's turmoil, Callie asked, "How are you balancing everything?"

"I don't know. I mean, I'm not handling things well." Alex stammered. "I don't want to stop anything that is happening with her, believe me. Everything feels right. She feels right."

Callie watched her friend intently. "Then what's the problem?"

Alex continued with as much enthusiasm as she could muster, "The response from the FDA has been positive, and the team is on cloud nine with all of our progress." Alex grabbed Callie's hand as she continued,

"The threats have escalated, but Michael has assured me he has it under control." She said the words quickly and gave Callie's hand a quick squeeze.

Concern for her friend's well-being always an utmost priority, Callie stiffened but the look on Alex's face stopped her from saying anything. She stayed quiet, sensing there was more.

Alex twirled her wine glass. "I just thought I would feel differently. This is the day I've been waiting for, waiting so long for, you know?" Alex's eyes searched Callie's. "So why doesn't this feel good?"

Callie regarded her. "Alex, I've never seen you so out of sorts before. I don't even know what to say."

"I messed up, Callie. Even though I said I didn't want to, I think I'm reliving the same mistakes I made with Kate," confessed Alex.

"It is not too late. Tell her how you feel."

"She doesn't want to see me."

"You cannot give up that easily, Alex. If she is who you want, then you need to fight for her."

"But how? What should I do?"

"You need to tell her how you feel and keep showing her that she is important to you and that nothing matters more. You can't give up now, Alex. Not when you are this close to having something you've never had before."

"I'm afraid."

"Afraid of what?"

"Getting too close, telling her what I really want, not being able to give her what she wants, losing myself, losing my way. Take your pick."

"Sounds to me like you're finally finding your way," Callie said.

Alex bowed her head and let herself cry, "I am so tired of feeling not good enough."

Callie jumped up from her side of the booth to join Alex on hers. She put her arm around her shoulders and pulled her in for a bear hug. She kept a tight hold on Alex as she spoke. "It's time, Alex. It's time for you to let go of your need to control everything. You need to accept that you have no control over any of this. You are enough and you have always been enough. You just won't let yourself believe that."

Alex sat in silence for a few minutes, allowing Callie's words to sink in.

"What should I do?"

"You need to go to her."

"Okay, I will." Alex wiped the tears from her face. "So, tell me—"

"No, I mean go now. You need to go to her right now, before you lose your nerve." Callie pulled Alex from the bench seat and walked her to the door. "We can finish talking later. Now go," she said, pushing Alex outside.

Alex drove straight to Madison's apartment.

Madison answered the buzz from her intercom. "Alex?" Madison sounded surprised.

"Can I come up?"

"Um, it's not a good time," said Madison. Alex heard

another woman's voice say, "You want this on the table, babe?"

"You're not alone. I should not have come. I'm sorry," said Alex. Madison heard the panic in Alex's voice and called after her, but Alex didn't answer.

Alex sat in her car, shrouded in darkness, and cried. She could not make herself drive away. And besides, Callie would never forgive her if she had to tell her she left without talking to Madison. This time *was* different. Madison was right. Alex didn't want her life to be just about the work she did. Alex wanted someone to share her life with. The mistakes she made with Kate were clearer to her now, but was it already too late for her and Madison? "It can't end like this." Alex said it out loud to help convince herself. *You cannot run away again. You have to tell her how you feel. You have to make her understand.*

Alex waited, hoping the woman Madison was with was not spending the night. Almost an hour later, she saw a woman, who looked a lot like Rachel, leave Madison's apartment building. Her inner voice shouted, *It's now or never.*

As soon as Madison answered the intercom, Alex blurted out, "Before you tell me to leave, I need to talk to you. I need to try to explain. Please let me come up."

"Alex, have you been out there this whole time?"

"Yes. I waited for your friend to leave." Alex yanked on the door handle as soon as she heard the click of the lock and rushed to Madison's floor. Madison was standing in the open doorway waiting for her when she arrived.

"Were you with Rachel?" Alex asked, even though she was afraid to have her suspicions confirmed. "Are you back together?" Alex looked at Madison and felt an unsettling pang of jealousy.

"Yes, Rachel was here. No, we are not back together," replied Madison. Alex felt only a slight bit of relief as her words sank in.

"I don't like it," Alex said out loud.

"Well, you have no right to like what I do or don't do, or who I do it with. You made it clear I was just in your way, keeping you from what you hold most precious." Madison's words sounded harsher than she meant them to, making her realize she had been denying how raw her own feelings still were.

"I'm sorry. I didn't come here to upset you. Can we go inside and talk, please?"

Madison moved to let Alex in. She motioned to the couch. "Do you want a drink?"

"No, thank you."

Before Alex could lose her nerve, she said, "I was wrong, Madison. You were right. All these weeks without talking to you or seeing you, without being able to touch you or feel your touch is driving me crazy." Madison's unwavering expression told Alex she was not going to be convinced easily.

"You say that now but how can I trust this is how you really feel? Just a few weeks ago you were sure I was getting in your way."

"Because I have been in a similar situation before. With Kate. And I know what I need to do differently now."

"How so?" asked Madison.

"I treated Kate as a distraction, and I honestly thought I was doing the right thing. I thought I was right to put my work first, because I knew it had real potential to make a difference for a lot of people. Kate walked away, and I let her go without so much as a phone call. I was so distant I didn't even realize she was unhappy until the day she left.

"I remember that night like it was yesterday. The house was eerily quiet when I got home, and I could tell something was off, but I couldn't quite place what it was. I called out for Kate but was greeted with only silence. I went to the bedroom and found the closet doors open and a row of empty hangers. That's when it hit me. All of Kate's clothes were gone. I looked around again and saw that everything of Kate's was gone."

Alex recalled the realization that came crashing down on her like an unsuspected wave. It swallowed her up and rolled her over and smashed her against the sandy bottom. She struggled for breath, gasping for air. She remembered feeling a heaviness in her body as if she had been pummeled with wave after wave. She collapsed on the edge of the bed.

"I was exhausted and when I reached up to the pillows to pull the comforter around me, I saw a piece of paper with my name on it. It was in Kate's handwriting. She wished for me to find someone who brought a smile to my face and sent my pulse into overdrive by the mere sight of them, to find someone who made it hard for me to concentrate, or to complete thoughts when they looked at me, to find someone who made being close, enough. She wanted me to find someone I didn't know how *not* to want, like I had been for her." Alex shifted in her seat and grasped both of Madison's hands. "I convinced myself I wasn't capable of having that kind of connection with anyone. That is, until I met you."

Madison took a deep breath, "This is a lot to process, Alex. I've been trying to get you out of my head for the past several weeks, and here you are reopening wounds that have barely started to scab over. You told me you didn't want to hurt me, Alex, but you already have." Madison's words sliced through her.

Alex tugged on Madison's hands to pull her closer, but Madison resisted. "What's changed?"

"Me. I've changed, Madison. Please give me a chance to prove it to you."

"Are you sure I'm what you want?" Madison's gaze locked on hers.

"I am. I want everything you are willing to offer me." Alex arched her eyebrow as she spoke the words. She pushed Madison against the cushions and hungrily covered her mouth with her own with a newfound sense of possessiveness.

Alex's sudden dominance carried away Madison's urge to resist, and she gave in. She gave in to the excitement she felt when Alex took what she wanted.

When they parted, Alex looked at Madison, eyes full of hope and promise and said, "Please, Madison."

"I'll need some time to catch up."

"I wouldn't want it any other way."

Chapter *Eleven*

Monday

Seated at her desk on Monday afternoon, Alex's thoughts drifted to Madison as she gazed out the window. Madison was giving her a second chance, something that was new territory for her. She wasn't sure what those words meant or what she should do with them. Kate's note had been so clear that she was walking away, that she was done, and it had invoked such an overwhelming feeling of being her final word that it had never occurred to Alex to argue, to try to fight to get her back. She had just pushed her feelings of rejection and abandonment away and focused her attention back on her research. She had moved on.

But looking back on it, and seeing it play out more as a third party, she could be more objective. She had just accepted Kate's words, words on a paper note for Christ sake. Alex had just thought about herself and allowed her self-deprecating feelings to consume her. What had Kate felt? She would never know because she had never asked. Sitting there in that moment she felt a wave of sadness for Kate, and she felt disgusted with herself. In her head, she heard the words, *You're such a dick.* She straightened in her seat and took in a long, slow breath. She could hear her former therapist's voice say, "In for four, hold for five, out for six."

She didn't want to mess things up with Madison like she had with Kate. "What to do?" she murmured out loud as she tapped her pen to her lips. She wanted to do something special. Madison had left that morning to vacation at her beach house. Should she send flowers or a gift to the house? Make reservations at a nice restaurant for them on her return? Her mind wandered.

Trevor popped his head into her office as he passed by her door and saw her staring out the window with a pensive look on her face. His brow furrowed as he entered the room.

"Are you daydreaming?" he asked. A slight grin began to tug at his lips. It took a moment for Alex to be pulled from her trance and notice Trevor.

"What's wrong with your face?" asked Alex.

"Sorry, I've just never seen you daydreaming before. Frequently head down, eyes laser focused on your laptop, yes, but gazing out the window, no."

Alex searched for seemingly foreign words. "Sit, I need your help."

He remained standing like a statue and his expression

morphed into disbelief. "And now something I've never heard before."

"Sit," she said more emphatically, and he obeyed. She was unsure about how to start.

"How can I help you, Miss Bennett?" Trevor saw the look of uncertainty cross her face and genuinely wanted to help her. He leaned forward in his seat.

Alex felt the heat travel up her neck and onto her cheeks. She forged ahead, ignoring her inner voice instructing her to shut it down.

"I need help coming up with something special to do for," she paused to find the right word, "for a friend of mine."

"A friend? Okay, what's the occasion? What were you thinking so far?" Trevor asked, fully engaged.

She's more than a friend, isn't she? I think I may be in love with her. Oh god. Alex had to silence the talking in her head. Trevor watched her internal struggle and the need to give her the answer overpowered him.

Hesitantly, he said, "I think maybe it's a whole lot of someone's got you wrapped around her little finger."

"What do you mean?" Alex blurted out, and felt the heat on her cheeks now burning.

"Your friend? We are talking about Madison, right?" Alex stared at Trevor but said nothing. "It's fucking awesome someone's finally grabbed your attention."

Alex's expression turned to one of shock at his use of language but she just grinned. "Is it that obvious?"

"Sorry, Alex, but I knew you were in trouble the day she walked into your office and I saw the look on your face when you sat down across from her."

Alex dropped her head and let out a long sigh as she recalled the meeting and Madison's blond hair pulled back off her face, the way her perfume reached for her like sweet tendrils, and her blue eyes that seemed to bore a hole right through her.

Trevor went into action. "How much time do we have to plan?"

"She's on vacation for a couple weeks."

"So why are you still here then?"

"What do you mean?"

"You said you wanted to plan a surprise for her," said Trevor. Alex looked at him blankly.

Trevor chuckled, "Alex, you are so smart and sometimes so naive. YOU should show up and surprise her."

"You mean me? *I* would be the surprise?" Alex asked.

"Yes, Alex. I've seen the way she looks at you too. Especially when you aren't looking. I'm going to go out on a limb here and say you showing up on her vacation would be the exact surprise she would want."

Alex entertained the thought for a minute. This week would be focused on completing the therapy protocol and beginning patient subject interviews. Technically, Patricia and the team could handle that part without her. *Should she?*

Trevor smiled as if reading her thoughts and nodded his head to acknowledge the silent question she posed. Callie's "Here's to trying new things" challenge rang in her ears.

Alex stood and said, "You'll take care of my calendar?"

Trevor was already out of his seat and walking back to his desk.

In her car several minutes later, Alex punched the address into her GPS navigation. *No turning back now.*

Five hours later, Madison opened the front door to her beach condo, glass of wine in hand, to find Alex standing there.

"What are you doing here?" Madison asked in a shocked voice.

"I wanted to surprise you." Alex held her breath waiting for Madison's reaction, hoping to God Trevor had been right.

Madison's smile and the way she looked at Alex touched her very soul, and Alex felt its warmth spread through her chest. She felt tears threatening to escape. She was thankful Madison backed away from the doorway at that moment to allow her to enter. She regained her composure as she followed Madison to the kitchen.

Madison poured Alex a glass of wine and walked through the living room and out onto the deck without another word. Alex followed like an obedient child.

Outside, Alex took a moment to scan her surroundings. The full moon illuminated the deck, the dunes, the ocean beyond them. Alex felt the pounding in her chest as the waves crested and landed against the beach and the water hissed and dissipated as it crawled along the friction of the sand. The smell of salt was strong. The light breeze brought the ocean mist to her, thinly coating her face and exposed skin with a tacky residue.

Alex turned away from the mesmerizing waves to look at Madison sitting quietly on the wicker loveseat. "Is it okay that I'm here? You haven't said anything." Alex sat down next to Madison and searched her face.

"I'm just a little shocked. I can't believe you are really here. You said you had so much work to do over the next several weeks."

"And I have a great team of people who can do what needs to be done, so I can be where I need to be, here with you." Alex reached out to cradle Madison's face in her hands as she lightly kissed her.

Madison reached for a blanket from a nearby chair and threw it over their legs to ward off the gusts of cool air that swirled around them. They sat in a comfortable silence and listened to the waves break on the shore. Each long, inhaled breath of the sea seemed to eliminate more and more of Alex's stress that had accumulated over the last several months.

Alex closed her eyes and tilted her head back against the loveseat. She had not been certain of her choice to come, but now she felt confident she had made the right decision. She turned her head to see Madison smiling at her. The wind teased strands of her hair. Alex reached out to tuck a lock of it behind Madison's ear. Would she ever tire of the caring look Madison gave her or the feelings it stirred in her? The warmth in her eyes turned sensual. Madison was stunning. She squelched her physical needs before they threatened to distract her from her primary purpose to somehow find a way to explain herself.

She wound herself up and blurted out, "I want to tell you something I've never shared with anyone else before. I've been rehearsing this in my head the whole drive here, and if I don't get it out, I'll lose my nerve." Alex took a deep breath, and Madison shifted to face Alex.

"When I lost my dad . . ." Her speech faltered as she searched for the words. "He was my best friend."

Tears suddenly welled in her eyes, and she looked down at her hands clasped in her lap. A twinge of physical pain struck Madison when she saw the raw hurt on Alex's face. She reflexively reached for her and placed her hands over Alex's.

"He was my teacher. He was my confidant. He was my guide and protector. I went to him when I was happy, when I was sad. I told him my secrets. I told him my fears. He made me feel safe, like nothing could touch me." After a moment, Alex looked at Madison. Her palms were clammy and her ears ringing. Her tongue stuck to the roof of her dry mouth as she tried to lick her lips to continue. "You make me feel that same way, and it scares the hell out of me. I loved him, and he was taken from me. If I love you . . ." Her voice cracked and trailed off.

It took all Madison had in her not to say something to sooth Alex, but she remained still except to squeeze Alex's hands tighter.

"After we lost him, Mom sent me to a counselor to help me deal with my grief. She told me I had to find a way to escape getting stuck in the endless loops of thoughts in my head that just kept replaying his death over and over again, reminding me that he was no longer around and that I had lost him. I poured myself into school and then into my research. I became good at compartmentalizing my feelings, and I learned how to function effectively again. I trained myself so well, in fact, that it became my way to deal with everything. I created a room for things I didn't want to deal with and closed the door on them. I left them there and went back to my research. Keeping feelings and people at a distance kept me from getting hurt again.

"I've been afraid to truly let anyone in for fear of them leaving me, and so I keep people at a distance. I've never been able to commit to anything other than my research, and I've made it work, until now. Until you. I'm not okay with my status quo anymore. I want nothing more than to completely open up with you, but I don't have everything figured out yet. Will you help me? Could we maybe work on this together?" Alex desperately searched Madison's face as if the answers would appear there if she looked long enough.

Glimpsing sight of a younger version of the woman seated in front of her, trying to find her way, Madison wanted to wrap her in her arms and tell her everything was going to be okay. Madison's voice was soft when she finally spoke. "What I find so fascinating is that even as children we make decisions on how we see the world and how we'll react to it. Even more mind boggling is that as adults we sometimes forget that we have the power to change those perceptions formed in childhood as well as our reactions to them. To choose a different path, you have to let go of those earlier conceived constructs of how the world works and to how you respond to them. Am I making any sense?"

"It makes a lot of sense, yes." Alex wiped her hands across her eyes.

"You really want to take the risk with me?"

Alex nodded. "I do."

"I do, too."

Tears threatened as the implication sunk in, and Alex was overwhelmed with feelings for this compassionate, fascinating, and complex woman. Madison reached for Alex and pulled her closer. Alex shifted to curl up beside Madison and put her head in her lap. Madison rested a hand on Alex's head and lightly stroked her hair. Mentally exhausted, Alex fell asleep.

The smell of coffee and bacon brought Alex out of her slumber. The sun was shining on her face, and when her eyes opened enough to see her watch, she saw that it was eight o'clock. She looked around the room. She was alone. She didn't remember asking if she could stay over, let alone going to bed last night. She pulled the covers to the side and looked down to see she was clothed in only her underwear and a tee-shirt. And the tee-shirt wasn't hers. It made her groan out loud. Then the conversation from the evening before came flooding back to her, and she grimaced as the immediate discomfort surfaced. *Had she shared too much?*

She found Madison in the kitchen. Madison said, "Morning. Do you want some coffee?"

"Please," Alex said. Madison set a warm mug in front

of her as Alex took a seat at the bar.

"How did you sleep?"

"Like a rock actually." She tugged on her tee-shirt and asked, "Did we? How did I get into this?"

Madison smirked as she took a sip of her coffee, "No, we didn't, but I put you in it. I thought it would be more comfortable than what you were wearing."

"Thank you. It obviously was." Alex looked sheepish. "About last night. I'm sorry. I was rambling."

Madison stopped in the middle of what she was doing and said, "Don't do that. Don't apologize to be accommodating or downplay the conversation. It's too important for us if we are to move forward." There was a sternness in Madison's voice that Alex had not heard before, and it made her stop short.

Alex bit her lower lip. "Okay."

Madison turned back to the stove. "Are you hungry? I made bacon and eggs."

"Yes."

Madison prepared a plate for each of them and took a seat at the bar. With her fork poised in front of her mouth, Alex said, "You know, you're kind of bossy."

Madison shot her a warning glance until she saw the smile on Alex's face.

"Eat, already. I want to spend the day on the beach." She paused before adding, "You are welcome to join me if you want to. I can give you something to wear."

That evening after dinner, Madison created a cozy

space in front of the fireplace and Alex joined her. Madison settled against the cushions and asked, "Will you tell me more about what happened with Kate?" Alex's habitual reaction to deflect surfaced like clockwork, but she stopped herself when she heard Madison's words from this morning on replay telling her not to push her thoughts and feelings away because working through them was important. *Okay, we're really doing this.*

"Kate and I met when I moved my horses to the barn where she taught horseback riding lessons. I took lessons from her, and we started spending more time together. We liked a lot of the same things. We both had an inner drive to succeed. We fit well together."

Alex paused as she reflected before she continued. "We both worked a lot, but toward the end of our relationship, I was working all the time. I didn't make a conscious effort for us, and that's when it started falling apart. I can see that now when I look back on it. At the time, when she left, it felt like a slap in the face. No warning, no call, nothing. I realize now that she had been pulling away little by little for some time, and I didn't see it. It dawned on me much later that I was physically present, but I wasn't actively engaged with her."

Madison didn't say a word.

Redirected in her thought process, Alex blurted out, "I have a confession to make. I didn't know what to say to you when you were waiting for me at my house that night. I was having déjà vu when you were talking about making life truly worth living by surrounding yourself with loving family and friends. Kate used to ask me to spend more time with her. She used to tell me that the relationships we built and maintained were the ultimate gifts in life. You made me question myself that night, Madison, and you were right.

"I don't spend enough time with the people I care about even though I convince myself that I do. I know my research is important, and I hope that it will help a lot of people in the long run. But I have been so focused on helping strangers that I have been neglecting the people who matter most to me. My family and friends in my inner circle need me too." Alex voiced a revelation that seemed to occur to her at that very moment. "Do you know what I find so ironic? The very thing I work so hard to protect for others is the single thing I neglect most in my personal life. How's that saying go? You can't see what is right in front of your face."

"May I share an opinion?" Madison asked. Alex nodded. "I think you have a rare gift, Alex. You have such an extraordinary inner drive that compels you to find the answers you seek. That drive is what makes you successful. You have found a way to focus your energy with such discipline on the task at hand that your surroundings blur, including the people there, and it's easy to lose sight of them. I would imagine the time you spend disengaged from those around you is directly related to the time it takes you to find the answers you seek. I think that as disciplined and as strong-willed as you are, you could bring everything in your periphery into focus, even when you are working on something important. If you concentrated on your awareness of it and, of course, if you're willing to."

Alex gave Madison the most loving look she could muster without actually saying the words out loud. *Still too chicken shit*, she told herself.

"Seriously, do you have any idea how absolutely amazing you are?" Alex asked.

Madison blushed and her beautiful smile lit up her face. Alex had trouble discerning whether Madison had read her thoughts or if it was her reaction to the compliment. Either way, she secretly relished the realization that she was able to elicit such a look from her. The one that made her feel like melting right there on the spot.

Alex smiled and said, "I think you missed your calling, Doc. You could have been a psychologist."

"Didn't you know that a pharmacist is a jack of all trades?" Madison chimed in with a deep, throaty laugh, something she had not done in a while. It felt good.

"May I ask you a personal question?" Alex asked, needing a break from her own cobwebbed mess of cerebral synapses.

"I think that is only fair."

"What happened with your relationship with Rachel?"

"Things were really great for a while. We had similar interests, and we both enjoyed sharing time between staying home and traveling. Then I broached the subject of starting a family, but she didn't want to. I hoped she might change her mind, but after a year or so, I realized that wasn't going to happen with her, so I broke it off."

"You want children?" Alex asked, with more surprise in her voice than she had intended.

"I did. But I've resigned myself to the fact that I'm

not getting any younger and children may not be in the cards for me."

"I'm so sorry, Madison. You deserve everything you want."

Alex's features held such sincerity that Madison had to look away. Madison's resignation had been firm, but it was on the verge of cracking. *Alex doesn't know what's in her eyes. She has no idea what it's like to be on the receiving end of that look.* Could Madison dare to hope for a future with Alex when Alex struggled to define her own feelings?

Wanting to regain Madison's gaze, Alex moved to kneel in front of her. Madison searched Alex's face and secretly gambled on what to do.

"Don't hurt me, Alex."

"Never," Alex whispered softly.

Throwing caution to the wind and giving into the undeniable electricity pulsing between them, Alex brazenly bridged the remaining space separating them, connecting with a sensuous kiss. Alex closed her eyes to lose herself in all that was Madison. Her senses were ignited as she fell into Madison's inviting embrace. She savored the lingering hint of wine from her soft lips. She took in a deep breath of her intoxicating perfume. It enveloped her like a sheer blanket, and it made her feel safe.

As their kiss deepened, Alex repositioned herself and pressed her body more fully against Madison. She gently nudged Madison's knees apart so she could nestle herself between her legs. A deep groan escaped Madison when Alex moved her hips against her core. Madison ran her fingers through Alex's hair and cradled her neck to pull her even closer, wanting to taste more of her, to feel more of her. She ran her hand under Alex's shirt to feel her skin. Madison circled Alex with her legs and Alex felt her heated center against her stomach. Her gut tightened and her pulse quickened. Madison's hands traveled across her shoulders, down her back, to her sides, exploring and rediscovering.

All of Alex's nerve endings were on high alert, pulsating one message after another to her brain and back, making it difficult for Alex to distinguish one from the other as Madison moved from one area of her body to the next. Alex pulled her body away to give herself just enough access to the buttons on Madison's shirt and to rid herself of her own. Alex was delighted to find bare skin and she trailed her hand over Madison's stomach and up over her breasts and tugged at her bra, desperate to be free of anything between them.

Madison matched her desire, unbuttoning Alex's jeans and tugging them down her thighs. Once set free and unencumbered by their clothing, their hands resumed their search. Madison wasted no more time and boldly ran her fingers through Alex's hot center. Alex hissed and bit down on her lower lip.

"Jesus," Alex's breath caught in her throat, and when Madison leaned in, Alex felt soft lips caress her ear.

"Breathe, sweetheart," Madison whispered.

Basking in the feel of Alex and nearing her own breaking point, Madison forced herself to still and said, "Alex, please tell me you're not going to run away this time."

An uncontrollable wave of untamed emotion flooded through Alex's body as her words registered. *God no, I think I'm in love with you.* Her inner voice called out so loudly in her head that Alex was certain Madison had heard it. Her insecurities and doubts were loosening their grip on her and in that moment, she felt herself letting go. She felt more whole than she ever had before, and it offered her a heightened sense of fulfillment. She accepted it.

"I'm not going anywhere, baby," she exhaled in a husky voice. "Now, please finish what you started." The desire in her voice was thick and heavy.

The sound of Alex's words and the intense longing in Alex's dark eyes finished igniting the fire on Madison's already heated skin, threatening to consume her. Without speaking or giving up eye contact, Madison ran her fingers through Alex's thick arousal and resumed circling her swollen mound of flesh before sliding over it and slipping deep inside of her.

Alex clung to this woman, not ever wanting to let her go, and the feeling didn't seem strange to her anymore, or even new. Their bodies fit so well together, as if they were cast from the same mold, and Alex felt a new level of confidence and overwhelming joy by the fact that Madison was willing to be patient with her. Everything in that moment felt right. Alex let out a long, throaty groan as she reached her orgasm.

When Alex opened her eyes Madison was watching her. She smiled but said nothing. Alex ran her hand up Madison's side until she reached the base of her neck.

She stopped there to trace the lines of her collar bone.

"You are so beautiful," Alex said.

Alex's gaze fell to Madison's lips, and she leaned in with one hungry kiss after another and then pulled away biting Madison's lower lip between her teeth. She watched as Madison's lip turned a darker red from her playful assault. She continued her exploration over Madison's body, tracing her figure from her neck to her waist and down her legs and up again leaving goosebumps in their wake. Alex kissed Madison's bare neck and breasts as her hands traveled. Madison's insides did a cartwheel as she felt Alex's hand travel down and over her bellybutton and between her legs. She caught her breath and dug her teeth into Alex's shoulder. Alex gently pushed Madison against the cushions and ran her tongue over her stomach and thighs leaving a trail of kisses as she went.

"And you feel incredible," Alex whispered against her thigh and raised her head to look up at Madison. Alex felt Madison shift under her to find more friction. Alex traced a hand up and down her thighs and all around her core, deliberately avoiding the one place Madison wanted her the most.

"Alex,"Madison moaned, and pushed her pelvis against Alex trying to find contact. Alex finally touched her.

"You are so wet. I want to taste you," Alex whispered, and her words alone threatened to push Madison over the edge. Alex satisfied her wanton desire to possess Madison until she pleaded with her to stop. She held onto Madison tightly as her whole body shuttered through her climax.

Madison's skin held onto a crimson hue as she rolled on top of Alex. "Your turn," Madison growled through clenched teeth.

Alex smiled and knew she was in trouble. Madison settled between her legs and ran the flat of her tongue over her slick folds. Alex took in a sharp breath and tried to slowly exhale. Madison expertly took her right to the edge of her orgasm, to begin the climb up, and then she slowed. Alex raised her hips to avoid losing the gratifying contact, but Madison continued to tease her with a lighter touch of her tongue.

"Maddie, please," Alex pleaded. Madison raised her head. Hearing her nickname emanate from Alex's lips in that delicious way did something wonderful to her insides.

"Don't stop," Alex pleaded again. A slow, seductive smile spread on Madison's face as she waited for Alex to look at her.

Madison's blue eyes had taken on a dark shade of gray and in a low, husky voice she said, "I like the way you say my name. Say it again and tell me what you want."

Alex felt a bolt of electricity traveling the length of her body that exploded in her core. Mesmerized, she begged, "Maddie, please take me."

Maddie did just that. She played Alex like a professional musician plays her instrument. Alex hadn't thought there was anything that could excite her more than watching Madison's body as she danced that night in the bar. But that feeling of anticipation was nothing compared to the way she made love to her. *Oh god*, Alex thought, *I may not survive this.*

Alex remained close by Madison's side for the next two days, leaving the bedroom only when their hunger could be satisfied by something other than their love making.

With the week nearing its end, Madison walked Alex to the door to say their goodbyes.

"I don't want to go," Alex said as Madison leaned in to kiss her.

"I don't want you to go either, but you have work and people waiting for you." Madison smiled and Alex nodded. "I'll be back in town at the end of next week."

Alex drove home replaying the glorious days and nights she and Maddie had spent together. After she had fed the horses and settled in for the night on the couch with Kenzie and Moose, she reached for her phone to send Maddie a text.

"I want to come back. I miss you already," she typed.

Several minutes later her phone chirped with a reply, "Ditto."

Chapter *Twelve*

Friday

Alex returned to the office to face a lot of people anxious as to her whereabouts. She had never taken off like that before. It was so out of character for her. Her team's reaction ran the gamut from concern to shock. Trevor had purposefully not forwarded her email or phone messages and inquiries to her cell phone. She appreciated being able to disconnect for a few days to focus solely on Madison even if it would take her days to crawl out of an exorbitant pile of emails and return phone calls.

With a smirk on his face, Trevor sashayed into Alex's office when she returned from her morning team meeting, "So?"

Alex looked up from her laptop and tilted her head, baiting him for the rest of the question.

"So, what happened?" Trevor asked as he flopped himself into a chair, busting at the seams in anticipation.

Anxious for a response, he added, "Tell me I was right."

Alex's expression softened as she conjured up the thoughts of their conversation which prompted her to go see Madison in the first place. She contemplated a moment on how much she should share. "Suffice it to say, you could not have been more right."

A smile traveled across Trevor's lips. "You're not upset with me about withholding your calls and messages?"

"I probably should be, but I'm not. Maddie and I needed that uninterrupted time together."

"You're calling her Maddie now?" Trevor's smile grew. Alex felt her cheeks flush as she recalled how and when she was compelled to use the nickname for the first time. She was relieved that Michael decided to interrupt them at that moment.

Michael marched right into Alex's office with no regard to the fact that Trevor was seated in front of her, and it was obvious they were in conversation.

"Where have you been? Where were you?" he barked his questions. Trevor took that as his cue to extricate himself from both the chair and the room.

"Hi to you too," Alex said, attempting to diffuse his red zone demeanor. He paced back and forth and tapped his fingers along the back of the chair Trevor had just vacated. "I was worried about you. Things have escalated, and I didn't know where you were. It scared me. You scared me." Michael finally took a seat.

"What things are you talking about?" Alex asked.

Evading her question, Michael said, "I'm placing a private detail on you, and I think we need to start escorting you to and from the office and possibly request a detail at your house at night."

"I don't understand what that means, Michael." Alex asked, thoroughly bewildered.

"I've heightened the threat level due to recent correspondence that has made its way into my hands. I want to play it safe by assigning a bodyguard to you."

"What kind of correspondence, Michael?" she asked, shooting him a no-nonsense look.

Judging by her facial expression, he decided to come clean with her. "Alex, we may have a real problem with a person or persons who have an adamant aversion to what your research could potentially lead to. Especially as far as taking rights away from patients and giving that authority to doctors and insurance companies when it comes to the use of gene tests during routine doctor visits and checkups."

"But we have no idea if that will happen in the future and that decision is not solely mine to make anyway," Alex argued.

"Unfortunately, that truth is irrelevant and bears no weight here, I'm afraid. Someone blames you and is holding you accountable for the outcome. It's all I have to go on right now, Alex. I would feel better if I knew you had someone with you all the time."

"It's not logical, but okay," Alex conceded.

"There's more. There's also been an attempt to breach our firewall. Luckily our security was more intelligent, and it was able to thwart the trojan horse. We are keeping a close eye on it."

Alex stared at Michael in disbelief.

"What time are you headed out? I'll introduce you to your new bodyguard before you leave today."

"Not early. I have a lot of emails to comb through and reports to review."

Michael got up to leave. "I'll leave you to it."

Alex's new bodyguard, Chris, stood six feet five and was a former football player, former cop who now worked for a private security firm. Alex had a hard time believing anyone would want to mess with him. When she could no longer look at another email, she texted him to say she was headed out. He texted her back that he would meet her in the building's lobby. He wanted her to drive her car home, and he would follow her. He then intended to stay with her and personally escort her back and forth to the office and anywhere else she would need to go she guessed. Until when, Michael hadn't said.

In the lobby, she told Chris she'd be stopping off to see Callie before heading home.

Alex's eyes adjusted to the lights as she walked into the bar. Callie wasn't in her usual spot behind the counter. Alex took a seat at their booth to wait, and Chris took a seat at the bar where he could keep an eye on her. She rubbed her temples trying to dissuade the headache forming behind her eyes. She looked up and watched Callie enter the room through the door marked "employees only." She was a sight for her sore eyes. Callie's gaze landed on her immediately. She set the box she carried at the end of the bar and made a beeline in her direction.

Callie sat across from Alex and reached for her hands. "I didn't know whether to sit tight or call out the troops to find you. I had to threaten Trevor before he caved and told me where you were."

Alex smiled. "He takes his matchmaker job very seriously." Alex's joke made Callie laugh.

Callie motioned to her bartender to bring them drinks and noticed Chris looking over at them. "Do you know the big guy sitting at the bar?"

"He is my new bodyguard."

Callie's eyes widened. She looked over at him again and then back at Alex. "And why do you need a bodyguard?" Callie felt the hair prickle on the back of her neck.

"Michael assigned him to me after raising the threat level."

Alex relayed the same information to Callie that Michael had shared with her earlier in the day. Callie took a big gulp of her beer.

"Listen, Callie. I'm sorry I didn't call you to tell you where I was. It took me the whole drive to the beach to work through what I wanted to say to Madison. To tell you the truth, I'm not even sure all that practice helped me much. I still had trouble putting the right words together."

"What happened?" Callie asked, hoping her uneasiness

about Michael's concerns didn't show up in her voice.

Despite her weariness from her first day back in the office, the conversation with Michael, and her looming headache, Alex's face lit up, and Callie saw the twinkle in her eyes, "Everything happened." Alex filled her friend in on the days she had spent with Madison, leaving out no details. Callie's eyes were wide as she soaked it all in.

"Wow!" Callie stared at Alex with a satisfied look on her face and took another swig from her beer. "And are we saying the 'L' word yet?"

"Not out loud yet, no."

"But you feel it, don't you?" Callie's expression was serious, and Alex nodded slowly. "Baby steps, then."

Alex appreciated that Callie knew when not to push her.

"Your turn. How are things going with Tina?" Alex asked.

"Really well. I've invited her to stay over a few nights now, and we've had the most amazing sex ever. Callie's cheeks flushed at her declaration.

"Are you seriously blushing right now?" Alex asked. Callie's cheeks never flushed because nothing embarrassed her.

Callie said, "I told you I like her."

"What? Callie's crushing? I never thought I'd see the day!" Alex gaped at her.

Callie fidgeted, clearly uncomfortable.

"Spill. What does she like to do? Does she have hobbies? Where does she live?" Alex doled out a handful of questions at once.

Callie tackled the barrage one at a time. "She loves being a cop, and I know she likes paintball and spending time outside, but I haven't been to her place yet."

"Why not?"

"I don't know," said Callie. "She's been meeting me at the bar and at my place after her shifts."

"So what? She's not opening up to you except in bed?" asked Alex. Alex felt an uneasiness settle in her gut.

Callie ignored her question and continued, "I want you to meet her, and it's way past time for me to meet Madison. What do you say to a double date next weekend?"

"I couldn't agree more. Let's do it."

Friday

Madison agreed to dinner with Callie and Tina the Friday night she returned from the beach. Alex had been running late, and she asked Madison to meet her at the restaurant. Callie was seated at the bar with a drink in hand when Madison arrived. Callie casually watched the attractive blond order a drink for herself.

"Madison?"

"Yes," she responded and smiled at the stranger.

"Hi. I'm Callie Mason, the best friend." She smiled as she moved a seat closer. "It's nice to finally meet you. I've heard a lot about you."

Madison laughed and said, "I hope good things." Her words slipped off her tongue like silk. Callie saw right away what had attracted Alex to her.

"Well, she tells me everything." She paused to appraise the effect her words had on Madison. She didn't catch even a slight change in her beautiful complexion, so she continued, "However, I have never seen Alex happier, and I think that has a lot to do with you. So, I would not be her best friend if I did not make you aware of the fact that if you hurt her, you will have to deal with me."

"Okay," Madison stated, matter of fact through a sly grin. "I am certainly glad we got that out of the way before the rest of our dinner companions arrive." Her tone took on a more serious note, "But I can assure you, I am not the one dealing the cards when it comes to Alex."

Callie liked this woman. "Alex can be very complicated, but she's worth it." She looked past Madison's shoulder to focus on Alex as she approached them.

"Speak of the devil, were your ears burning?" Callie asked as Alex bent and gave her a kiss on the cheek and turned to give Madison a kiss on the lips.

"I guess they should be burning since I see you two have met . . ." Alex's statement sounded like a question.

"We have," Madison responded.

Callie looked down at her phone and said, "Let's get a table. That was Tina. She's going to be about twenty minutes late. She has some paperwork to finish before she can leave work."

Tina arrived just in time for appetizers and gave the waiter her drink order. Callie stood to greet her and introduced her to everyone.

"I'm sorry I'm late," Tina said. "There is always so much paperwork to keep up with." She took a seat beside Callie and directly across from Alex.

"What do you do?" Madison asked politely. Alex looked at her and smiled as she realized how easy it was for Madison to create a comfort zone where others felt included and safe.

"I'm a cop." Tina answered.

"I would imagine that is a very tough job."

"It has its days, for sure," Tina commented. "And you? What do you do?"

"I'm a Pharmacy Director at the American Pharmacy Association. I oversee specialty medication continuing education programs for licensed Pharmacists," Madison answered.

"So, you are both in the medical field? You work at Biogenetics, right, Alex?"

"Yes, that's right." Alex confirmed employment but said nothing more to elaborate. Her disclosure agreement with the lab was very clear in its language not to divulge proprietary information. Over the years she had found it easier to avoid proactively talking about her job with strangers, especially when alcohol was involved. She stuck to answering direct questions only.

"I saw an article about your research." *And here we go*, Alex thought. "Cutting edge, it said. Amazing progress your team is making with breast cancer research." Tina held Alex's gaze.

Receiving the remark as a compliment, Alex said, "Thank you. It is nice to hear outside words of encouragement."

"I didn't say I agree with it or support it." Tina was quick with the retort and a hush fell over the table. "I'm in the camp of there are some things we are better off not knowing, our life expectancy being one of them. Knowing about a disease we'll get, maybe, sometime in the future is destructive. Some people can't handle knowing."

Tina looked around the table at everyone's shocked expressions and slowed her speech, "I just think everyone should be able to make their own choice, that's all." Tina picked up her beer and took a long swig of it.

Alex shot Callie a look and read her expression to tread lightly and to be nice, so Alex sought to stay neutral and hoped that by explanation she might extend an olive branch to soften Tina's opinion.

"I appreciate your point of view, Tina. Gene therapy has come a long way. Now that we know specifically what genes to target for certain diseases, it gives us a tremendous opportunity to develop preventative medications. Prevention can protect us from those diseases rather than only treat the condition after a diagnosis has been made as doctors currently must do. The hope is that we are able to give people more quality of life and avoid a lot of unnecessary pain."

"I don't agree," Tina responded and was about to say more when Callie reached for her hand. She stopped herself and looked around the table. "I'm sorry. We haven't even received our dinners yet, and I'm already overpowering the conversation with my opinions." Tina gave Callie a half smile and fell silent.

Idle chit-chat carried the foursome to the main course, but the initial tension remained. When the waiter delivered their meals and refilled their drinks, Alex was thankful the conversation moved onto less controversial subjects.

Halfway through their meal, Tina started another line of questioning and directed her question to Alex. "How did the two of you meet?"

Feeling a nagging ulterior motive based on Tina's previous questions, Alex decided to go the vague route with her response. She was not comfortable sharing personal details about herself or Madison. "A mutual friend introduced us." Alex's answer prompted a sideways glance from Madison.

"How long ago?" Tina asked in a way that felt more like an interrogation than friendly dinner conversation.

"It's been a few months. In fact, not long after you and Callie met, isn't that right, Callie?" Alex attempted to redirect the conversation. "Why don't you tell Madison how you met Tina."

Callie chimed in immediately. "Tina and I met at my bar. She came in after her shift one night with a couple of her colleagues, and she opened a tab. I got her name from her credit card, and here we are."

Madison said, "You must be a really good bartender." Her comment made the other three women laugh. Alex took that high note as an opportunity to call it a night, and Callie asked for the check.

Callie said, "My idea, my treat."

Alex was grateful that Chris had flown under the radar all night, but when they walked outside and he fell into step slightly behind her, Madison's question was plastered all over her face. Alex walked Madison to her car but not before asking Chris to hang back.

Alex said, "I have so many things I want to say to you, like how much I missed you, what a disaster dinner was, shit, that's time we'll never get back. I promise I can explain the brute," pointing over her shoulder to Chris, "but what I really want to say, or ask is, will you spend the day with me tomorrow?"

"Sweetheart, slow down." The smile on Madison's face widened. "I would love to." The endearment was not lost on Alex and hearing it outside of the bedroom made her heart leap around in an unexpectedly pleasing way.

"Great. Tomorrow's weather is supposed to be nice, so I thought we could take the horses out in the morning, relax in the afternoon, and then grill out for dinner. I thought we could enjoy the evening with drinks by the fire pit."

"Wow. That sounds wonderful."

"And, if you bring an overnight bag, I will make you breakfast Sunday morning," Alex added shyly. Madison's tired eyes searched Alex's face and Alex caught something fleeting in those stormy blues, but she couldn't pin it down.

"You don't have to do this," Madison whispered.

"I want to, Maddie. I don't want you to have any doubts about my feelings for you. Besides, it's way past time for me to start spoiling you."

"Okay then, I'm in." Madison straightened and Alex

leaned in and kissed her goodnight. "Get some rest, and I'll fill you in on everything tomorrow."

Alex dialed Callie's number on her drive home.

Diving right through pleasantries, Callie said, "I'm so sorry, Alex."

"Callie, what the fuck was that?"

"I have no idea what happened tonight. Tina didn't want to talk to me after dinner. She just took off." After a short pause, Callie added, "I did not want to say anything to you the last time we talked, but Tina told me she has been struggling with her counseling sessions and that her doctor keeps changing her meds. Nothing he gives her seems to be helping her."

"What have you told her about me?"

"You haven't been the topic of any of our conversations except to mention your name and that we are close friends. I am just as shocked as you are, Alex."

"Well, she did her homework on me, didn't she? She definitely had some strong opinions on the subject of my research. Her comments seemed well thought out and almost as if she came prepared to share her views about it."

Callie didn't say anything.

"You didn't tell me she was such a loose cannon. You think it's her meds?" asked Alex.

"All I know is that she's different when she's with me. I've never seen her go off like that before. You don't understand because you don't see the side of her I see when it's just the two of us," said Callie.

"Don't be naïve, Callie. If no one else sees that side of her, one of two things is happening. Either she's only being real with you, or the way she shows up for everyone else is who she really is and for you, she's putting on a show."

Callie lashed out. "I don't think you are the best person to be giving out relationship advice."

Alex took a deep breath to calm her nerves, "I'm sorry, I just get a bad feeling about this, Callie. Will you just promise me that you will be careful, please?"

"Always."

Chapter
Thirteen

Saturday

Alex heard a car pull into the driveway and when the dogs started crying at the door, Alex yelled, "Door is open, come on in."

Madison was dressed in her riding clothes. She walked in carrying a bag. She looked at Alex and then at the bag and said, "Overnight bag as requested" and flashed her gorgeous smile.

Alex said, "Lucky me! Coffee?"

"I would love some."

"It's almost ready," Alex said as Madison leaned in and kissed her.

They looked at each other for a moment before Madison looked around and said, "There must be something about the smell of coffee and standing here in the kitchen with you that turns me on," Madison teased.

"As I said, lucky me. I have a pot brewing all day long."

Alex laughed. "Please, sit. How do you want your coffee?" The thought occurred to her that they had shared coffee before, so why didn't she know how Madison took hers? Frowning, she realized that this was the first time she had made it for her. She felt a heaviness in her chest and the voice in her head said, *Be present.*

"Two sugars."

"Nothing else? Hmm."

"What?" Madison asked.

"Nothing, I just pegged you for lots of cream." She drew a baseless comparison between the number of ingredients added to coffee and the level of complexity of the personality who drank it. Her mind quickly equated black coffee to a plain jane, surface-level personality and a multi-ingredient, sugar plus cream plus even flavored shots to a complex, multilayered personality. She seriously needed to stop turning everything into a hypothesis test.

"Not in my coffee," Madison purred through a mischievous grin that made Alex giggle and her skin flush. How could she make discussing something as mundane as coffee sound so seductive?

Alex took a sip of her coffee as they walked to the table. "Where would you like me to begin?"

"How about with what happened at dinner last night? Madison asked. "Did you wrong that woman somehow in another lifetime?

"Your guess is as good as mine. I was floored by her comments."

"Is it possible the two of you have interacted and you just don't remember her?"

Alex shrugged her shoulders.

"Well, she is obviously not your biggest fan," Madison said.

"I'm disappointed the night didn't turn out like Callie and I had planned. We were really hoping for a chance to connect as couples. I'm sorry."

"No need to apologize to me. It is not your fault. Who was the big guy following you around?" Madison asked as she gave the dogs her attention.

"His name is Chris. Michael likes to play it safe."

"Is he supposed to stay here with you overnight?" She looked around, almost expecting to see him walk into the kitchen at any moment.

"He drives me back and forth to work, and he has his patrol buddies watch the house during the night." Alex explained.

"I don't know if I should feel afraid for you or relieved that you have protection. This situation is a new one for me, Alex. I'm honestly not sure how I feel about it," Madison admitted. Alex reached for her hands and caressed them under hers.

"Do what I do then. I concentrate on what I have control over, and that's my research. We all have a job to do and please know that Michael and Chris are really good at theirs."

Madison smiled, "That's very good advice, Miss Bennett."

Their morning ride extended into the early afternoon and since they had no agenda to follow, there was no rush to get back. They took their time riding through Alex's property and stopped to relax along the trail at a small clearing. Alex hopped off her horse and tied him to a tree. She helped Madison do the same. Down the hill from where Alex placed a blanket for them to sit, they could see one of the neighboring properties through the trees. Apart from that, they were nestled into an embankment that created a sense of privacy. The air itself seemed to be holding its breath. Nothing stirred around them. The only sounds that could be heard came from the horses as they moved around, shifting their weight on the dry leaves beneath them.

"I like to come here when I need a break," Alex said. "The peacefulness helps calm my mind."

Madison looked around. "I can see why. It's beautiful here." She looked at Alex over her shoulder and studied her profile and waited for Alex to look at her.

"Thanks for inviting me today. I'm having a good time," Madison said.

"Thank you for agreeing to come." Alex smiled at her.

"It's nice to see this side of you, out here, surrounded by the woods and with your horses. You seem very happy here," Madison commented.

"I am happy here. Ever since I was a little girl, I wanted my own horse farm. It didn't need to be fancy, it just needed to be." Alex looked around them. "This place totally exceeded my expectations. I was living in the city when my mom called and told me about it. The timing was perfect since Kate had recently moved out of our apartment. Mom thought it was a sign and a way for me to move on."

"Was she right? Have you been able to move on?" Madison's gaze searched Alex's for the answer to a much deeper question.

Déjà vu. It took all she had not to look away. She felt laid bare, right here, out in the open.

Alex swallowed, hard. "Yes, I have. And honestly, if the feelings I'm developing for you are any indication, I think I may be in trouble."

Madison reached for Alex's hand and said, "I think I know what you mean."

"You do?"

"Yes."

Madison leaned in and kissed Alex softly on the lips. From this proximity Alex noticed how the bright sky lightened the blue in Madison's eyes. A few strands from her ponytail framed her face. Madison had a beautiful complexion that Alex was a little jealous of. Her lips held such an inviting softness about them. And her smile was one of a kind. When Madison looked at her with a smile that reached her eyes, Alex's whole body reacted. Her attraction to this woman was so great that she found it hard to sit still and not touch her in some way.

But the attraction was so much more than physical. She was drawn to her intellect and mesmerized by the positive energy Madison exuded. Alex felt good being around Madison, and she liked the person she was becoming with her. Her heart felt bigger somehow. A warm sensation spilled over her and sent a tingling, electric current down her limbs. *I love you*, she confessed to herself. The words were on the tip of her tongue, and she desperately wanted to say them out loud. Tears welled behind her eyes, threatening an avalanche down her face, and her mouth went dry. She opened her mouth to speak.

"I am not being a good host, am I? I have not fed you yet. Are you hungry?" *Coward*, she scolded herself.

Madison smiled and said, "I could eat," and then laughed. The sound of her laugh soothed Alex and the nagging voice in her head was replaced with Callie's supportive voice, "Baby steps."

"I love your laugh. It's contagious, and if I'm being totally honest, it does strange things to my body," Alex said.

"Really? Promise to show me later?" Madison said.

"I do."

After returning to the barn and tending to the horses, they spent the rest of the afternoon talking, laughing, and listening to music. They continued their conversation, moving from one topic to the next, as they prepared dinner together. They opened a bottle of wine, mixed a salad, and grilled a couple of steaks. Madison set the table while Alex collected and lit the wood for the fire pit. They enjoyed their romantic dinner by the fire and afterward enjoyed another bottle of wine. With glasses almost empty, Alex stood and extended her hand to Madison.

"Spend the night with me?"

Madison smiled as Alex led her into the house.

Wednesday

"I miss you." Alex read the text message from Madison as she walked into her office. "Did you make time for lunch?"

Not seeing Madison at the office was bad enough, but her being out of town again was almost unbearable. She was attending her annual pharmacy conference that lasted all week.

With a smile she keyed her response, "Only if you are bringing me some." Her phone rang.

"Hi."

"Hi, Alex. I'm sorry I can't bring you something and," she paused, "one of our panelists got sick so I will need to fill in for him during the Friday afternoon session. I had to push my flight to Saturday morning. I'm so sorry I'll miss our date Friday."

Alex heard the sound of genuine disappointment in Madison's voice. Alex was filled with a sadness and happiness at the same time. The gravity of realizing how much Madison meant to her caused a lump to form in her throat and an ache in her chest.

"I miss you, Maddie." She swallowed the lump away and shook her head, "You're stuck with me Saturday then, yes?"

"Absolutely. Can't wait. Okay, I've got to go. I'll call you when I land." She hung up.

Alex stared at her phone and jumped when it pinged with another text message. She was disappointed when the message wasn't from Madison. *Jesus. Get a grip.*

The question was from Callie. "Can you stop by after work tonight?"

"Everything okay?" Alex quickly typed back.

"It's Tina. We talked, and I want to fill you in."

"Sure, see you around six."

Callie had their table outfitted with drinks and appetizers when Alex arrived at the bar. Alex slipped into the booth and within minutes, Callie did the same.

"Hey, what's going on?" Alex wasted no time with pleasantries.

Callie picked up her beer and took several long swigs. "Alex, Tina had a fiancée named Anne."

"Had?" Alex asked.

"She died."

Alex's mouth dropped open before she formed the words, "What? Wait, when?"

"Anne had a family history of breast cancer, and her doctor ordered the gene test to screen her for it. It came back positive. She struggled initially with the decision to even take the test and then struggled afterwards trying to deal with the results of the test. In fact, she became so distraught over the results she had herself convinced that she was going to get the most aggressive form of the cancer and that she would need a double mastectomy. Tina said there wasn't anything she could do to help her."

"The cancer was really that aggressive, and it killed her?"

"No, it's worse than that." Callie's voice shook.

"How do you mean? How could it be worse?" asked Alex, her own voice uneven.

"She committed suicide two years ago," Callie said.

Alex picked up her beer and drained it.

"There's more. Tina found her in their apartment. Anne had cut herself while Tina was at work."

"*Fuck*, Callie." They sat for a few moments studying each other. "Her behavior at dinner makes more sense now," said Alex.

Callie's face was pale. "That's when she mentioned you by name, Alex. Her exact words were, "If only Alex had been smarter and found a way faster, Anne would still be alive."

"Where is Tina now?"

"I don't know."

Alex looked over at the bar where Chris was sitting. The expression on her face pulled him off his chair and both he and Todd were at the table in seconds.

"You need to call Michael, *now*." Alex tried to keep her voice calm.

Michael arrived at the bar within thirty minutes and the five of them huddled in the booth as Callie repeated their conversation for Michael's benefit. Alex couldn't peg the expression that flickered over Michael's face at the mention of Tina's name. She almost asked about it but stopped short when she was overcome by admiration as she listened to Michael take control of the situation. Somehow him knowing what to do next surrounded her with an invisible safety net, and it calmed her nerves.

"Chris, you're staying with Alex tonight. Don't let her out of your sight. Got it?" Chris nodded in complete understanding. He looked at Alex and then at Callie, "Maybe stay together tonight?"

After a quick glance at Callie, Alex said, "We'll stay at my house."

"Todd, go pack a bag. I'll feel safer if you're with us too," Callie added.

Michael removed himself from the booth and started tapping his phone.

"Where will you be?" Alex asked.

"I'm going to see my friends at the precinct. I'll check in with you later."

Saturday

Friday evening slowly rolled into Saturday morning. Michael had checked in with them several times during the evening. He had connected with the police, and he was confident they would get to the bottom of their concerns about Tina. The first light of dawn began evaporating the dark shadows in her bedroom, but Alex hadn't noticed. It had been well past two o'clock when she had fallen asleep. When her phone buzzed, she expected to hear Michael's voice again.

"Alex, Madison's been in an accident. You need to come to the hospital," Heather said.

"I don't understand. She was supposed to call me

when she landed this morning." Not fully awake yet, she struggled to process Heather's words.

"All I know is that she is in surgery now. Just come, okay? I'll meet you in the lobby of the Emergency Room," Heather pleaded.

"On my way."

Alex saw Heather as soon as she entered the Emergency Room lobby. Heather was leaning stoically against the wall, out of everyone's way, her arms folded across her chest. She looked up with a worried expression as Alex approached her. Alex was certain that she and Callie must look like something out of a movie, marching through the doors with their muscled sidekicks in tow.

Heather relayed what the nurse had told her so far, which wasn't much other than to say that Madison was in surgery and that the doctor would be out to see them as soon as they knew more. Heather motioned for Alex to follow her to the comfort room just down the hall where she had been directed to wait.

Alex took in the modest yellow room with sky blue plastic chairs lining two walls, two vending machines along the third wall, and a television, volume turned low, mounted on the opposite wall. In the center of the room were two couches, facing each other, with a coffee table placed between them. Stacks of magazines made a home on the table. Some appeared to have been there quite a long time with their wrinkled and worn corners and pages. Alex's attention was drawn to the rings left behind from the vending machine cups on several of the magazine covers.

She was overwhelmed by the importance and meaning of this simple room. The impact such an average looking room could have on the people who sat here and waited to hear the news about their loved ones was difficult to comprehend. Some, she would imagine, hearing good news, would forget the room entirely, while others, hearing bad news, may never forget it. She wondered which she would be. When her father died, there was no waiting for the doctor to tell them good news or bad news or results of surgery, or a prognosis for the future. It was just done. Her father was there that morning and gone by the afternoon. The paramedics on the scene called it D.O.A. Those words, dead on arrival, haunted her. Her family had not been afforded the luxury of hoping for an alternate outcome. At least with Madison there was hope for recovery. There was renewed hope for Alex too. When the dark thoughts that consumed her after her father died tempted her again, she pushed them away.

Heather walked over to an older woman seated in a blue chair by the windows. Heather introduced Alex to Madison's mother, Marie Thornton.

"Hello, Marie. I am Alex Bennett."

"I know who you are, dear. My daughter talks about you all the time."

"She does?" Alex asked, surprised.

"I know you make my daughter very happy," Marie said, as tears formed in her eyes.

"Well, she makes me very happy too. I am just sorry we are meeting under these circumstances. Would you like a cup of coffee?"

Alex listened as her change rattled through its path in the vending machine and waited for the paper cup to fill before she took a seat beside Marie. Some of the seats in the comfort room were occupied. Folks were huddled together in small groups. Two geriatric women were seated by themselves and a young man was seated next to a child who was crying. He had his arm draped around her and in a hushed voice appeared to be trying to console her.

After taking in her surroundings, Alex rested her gaze on Marie. Alex guessed she was no more than twenty years older than Madison. The years had been kind to her. It was clear where Madison got her striking features from.

"Thank you, dear," Marie said as she took the coffee. She noticed the worried lines on Alex's face. "She'll be okay. She's tougher than she looks."

Alex wanted to believe Marie's words, but they were unable to lift the sense of dread hovering over her.

"Marie, your daughter is the most amazing person I've ever met. She has helped me more than words can describe. I care about her, a lot."

"I can see that."

A couple hours later, Alex scored her second cup of coffee from the vending machine. Her attention had been so focused on Marie and the other people in the room when she arrived, she hadn't noticed the small table in the corner. *More magazines. More rings.* She decided to add the ring of her cup to a *Good Housekeeping* magazine, another memorial with those already there. They continued to wait.

A doctor finally walked into the room looking for them. Her face seemed to relay good news. *Thank god.* Alex suddenly realized she had been holding her breath every time a doctor walked into the room. The doctor told them that Madison was extremely lucky and that she was able to repair the internal damage caused when the ribs broke and properly set her rib and leg bones. A fragment from one of the broken ribs had punctured her right lung, so when she was brought into the emergency room, they had had to insert a chest tube to drain the blood from her lungs to keep her from suffocating. No one spoke and all eyes were glued on the small woman standing in front of them as she told them that with a lot of rest and some physical therapy, there was no reason that Madison would not make a full recovery. Alex was relieved to hear she could see Madison as soon as they moved her from the recovery room to a patient room.

Madison was still groggy from the anesthesia but noticed her mom as soon as Marie pulled a chair to the side of her bed. Marie picked up Madison's hand gently and kissed it. Heather moved around to the far side of the bed to give Madison a hug. Alex hung back to give Marie and Heather their space. When Madison looked back at her mom, she saw Alex standing behind her.

"Al-ex," she managed to say, as if two words. Marie shifted and motioned for Alex to move closer.

"You gave us quite a scare," Alex said. She squeezed Madison's forearm, desperate for the contact. She felt warm, and it helped to calm Alex somewhat. She took a deep breath.

Marie was the first to ask, "What happened, honey?"

Madison responded slowly, "I'm not sure. I braked to take the exit ramp off the highway, but nothing happened. The car didn't slow down, and I plowed right into the cars in front of me. I don't remember anything after that. I must have blacked out." A sudden look of fear crossed her face. "Am I okay?" Madison attempted to pull her head up to take an inventory of herself but winced in pain.

"Easy, dear," Marie said. "You are going to be fine. You didn't break anything that can't repair itself."

Madison tried to take a deep breath, but grimaced when her damaged lung and sore ribs allowed no more expansion. Her gaze moved from Heather to Alex, and she said, "Thanks for being here."

"Where else would we be?" Heather asked.

Alex wanted so badly to wrap Madison up in her arms and tell her everything would be okay. She brushed her thumb under her eye to catch a tear threatening to escape. "You get some rest, okay? We'll be here when you wake up."

Madison slowly let out a relieved sigh and drifted off to sleep.

Alex spent the rest of the night and the next day

sitting by the bed watching over Madison. They held short conversations as Madison would fall in and out of sleep. During the times Madison was asleep, all Alex could think about was how lucky she was to have Madison in her life. In fact, it was hard for her to remember her life without Madison in it.

A nurse walked into the room with a bouquet of flowers and set them on the side table.

Madison slyly looked at Alex and said, "You are here, so who are they from?"

Nice one, Alex. Someone beat you to it. Alex stood and reached for the card. Madison's room number was neatly printed on the outside of the envelope. She flipped it over to expose the card nestled inside. She stopped.

"What is it, Alex?" Madison asked with a hint of uneasiness.

Alex suddenly felt bile rising in her throat and reread the card, "AB—You did this. My turn to take something from you. You should have done your job faster."

Chapter
Fourteen

Monday

Alex pulled her car into the hospital parking lot. She put the car in park and turned off the engine. She sat quietly, enjoying the silence the enclosed space provided her, and reflected on the last few weeks. Her Phase 1 trials were going well with zero hiccups. Madison was recovering from surgery on par with her doctor's expectations. She should feel fortunate, and yet she couldn't shake the nagging uneasiness in her gut she'd had since the evening in the bar when Callie shared her last encounter with Tina. No one had heard from or seen Tina since then. And the flowers. Alex had not done a great job glossing over the card. But Madison had to focus on getting better right now. Alex wasn't going to pull her into her drama.

Her gaze shifted, and she saw Chris standing by the

curb waiting for her. She realized she was running later than usual this morning, so she dialed Trevor to let him know what time to expect her.

Alex and Chris boarded the elevator in the lobby to make their way to Madison's floor. She caught sight of Michael through the closing doors. He had been standing behind a column at the far corner of the lobby, with his back to her, but he shifted his position and she could see he was talking to someone. As the elevator doors closed, Alex saw the woman's profile. It looked a lot like Tina.

"What the fuck?" Alex muttered.

Chris looked at her. "What is it?"

"It's Michael. I think I just saw him in the lobby talking to Tina."

"Go to Madison's room and stay there. I'll find Michael," Chris said. He ushered her out of the elevator and down the hall before turning toward the stairs.

Alex was relieved to find Madison propped up in bed. Her hair was freshly combed and pulled back off her face, and some of the color had returned to her cheeks. She and Heather were talking. Heather had just made her laugh. Alex missed the sound of Madison's voice and her laugh. Her laugh always made you want to join in, even if you didn't know what you were laughing about.

"Hi," Madison said through her cheeky grin when Alex entered the room.

"Good morning. How are you feeling?" Alex gently

took Madison's hand in hers and placed a delicate kiss on her lips.

"Like I was hit by a truck. It's hard to breathe, and I ache all over, but I'll be okay. I'm glad you're here."

"Don't worry. I'm not going anywhere."

"Why don't I leave the two of you alone? I'll check in on you tomorrow, okay?" Heather said.

"I'll walk you out," Alex said. "I'll be right back, Madison." Alex pulled the door closed behind her as they left the room. "Would you be able to come back later today to check on her?" Alex asked.

"Why? What's going on?"

"I just want to be sure Madison has someone with her for the good part of the day."

Heather scanned Alex's face, clearly not believing her, "Alex, seriously, what's going on?"

Alex relented, "I don't want to alarm you or Madison, but I don't think her car accident was an accident."

"What do you mean?" Heather asked.

"I don't know all of the facts yet, but the authorities are investigating what happened. I just want to be sure one of us stays with Madison around the clock to keep a watch out."

"What am I watching out for?" Heather asked with growing concern.

"Call me if a police officer by the name of Tina Ramirez shows up. And don't let her into Madison's room, okay?"

Heather said, "All right. I'll come back after lunch."

"Thanks, Heather," Alex said and slipped back in

Madison's room. Moments later, Chris and Michael walked into the room.

"Found him," Chris stated.

Alex wasted no time before addressing Michael. "Can I talk to you? In private. Just some last minute work stuff, Madison. We'll be right outside."

Without a word Alex led Michael down the hall, far enough away so Madison couldn't overhear them but stopping before turning the corner so she could keep the door to Madison's room in view.

"You were talking to Tina," she hissed. It was an accusation and not a question. "I saw you with her in the lobby."

"That conversation had nothing to do with you, Alex," Michael fired back. Stunned, Alex took a step backward as if he had struck her.

"Is she the friend going through a rough patch, the one who has been monopolizing your time lately?" Alex asked. In her experience, you needed to pay attention to coincidences, good or bad. Michael's silent response only put her exasperation into overdrive.

"What the actual fuck, Michael! She could be the person threatening all of us."

Michael immediately broke, pain etched all over his face. "I don't believe that. Tina is my late sister's partner," Michael answered. "And yes, to answer your question, Tina is the woman I mentioned in conversation. She has struggled tremendously since Anne's death, and I've been trying to be there for her, to provide support in any way I can."

"Anne was your *sister*?" Her tone softened immediately. "Oh, I am so sorry, Michael." Alex sighed, feeling confused and terrified at the same time. "How is it that I didn't know you have—had—a sister and how is it that I didn't know she died?"

Michael said, "Well, we don't really talk much when we spend time together outside of work."

Alex nodded, fully appreciating that statement of truth. But more than that, the painful realization that slowly hit her was that she didn't *make* the time to really get to know the people around her. *You are a terrible person, Alex.*

"How do you know about Anne?"

Alex's voice was now calmer. "I met Tina through Callie. They started dating a few weeks ago and recently Madison and I went to dinner with them. Tina was pretty quick to share her views about my research. Callie called me a few days ago with concerns that Tina may be holding some kind of grudge toward me because of Anne's death. That's when we called you to join us at the bar. That nagging feeling returned when she recalled the fleeting look that had flashed across his face that night when Callie had said Tina's name. He knew Tina, he knew her well, in fact.

"What was she doing here, Michael? She's not returning any of Callie's calls or text messages, but now she shows up here at the hospital. Is Madison in danger?" Alex's voice was strained.

The look on Michael's face sent a shiver down Alex's spine.

"I don't know." He dropped his head and his shoulders sagged. Alex had never seen him look so defeated. She had always seen strength and power in him, and his commanding presence gave her confidence. He was always so sure of himself. Until now.

"Where is she, Michael?"

"I honestly don't know. She ran off when Chris approached us." Clinging to a last thread of hope, he added, "Her stories don't always make sense, and I have always found her to be a little odd, but Tina wouldn't hurt anyone. Even in front of my sister, she would sometimes go off on a tangent, and my sister would just look at me and roll her eyes. I started shrugging it off too.

"After my sister died, Tina wanted to spend more time with me. She doesn't have close family and has very few friends. I meet her for lunch or drinks every month or so to check in on her. She has struggled with Anne's death. And since the second anniversary of her passing, she's been having an exceptionally hard time with Anne being gone. Over the past six months her behavior has become more erratic. I drive her to her counseling sessions to make sure she goes. Her doctor struggles to get her maintained on a healthy medication regimen. When I asked her what was going on, she reluctantly told me she had stopped taking some of her meds."

"But, Michael, is she capable of trying to hurt someone thinking somehow it would help Anne?"

"No, of course not. She's just trying to deal with her grief." He fell silent and some of the color that usually painted his cheeks drained from his face.

"What is it, Michael?"

"Could Tina have orchestrated *all* of this?" Michael asked himself out loud in disbelief.

"Michael, you are scaring me. What are you talking about?"

"Anne used to tell me how unfair it was that her doctor ordered a gene test when she couldn't even handle the possibility of being at risk for breast cancer. We talked about how unfair it was that there wasn't a cure yet. This whole time I've been thinking the threats are coming from someone like Anne. A potential breast cancer victim. But what if Tina feels the same way? What if she thinks that interfering with your research will somehow right a wrong?"

Alex watched Michael intently.

"Tina told me she was here this morning to take a statement from a car accident victim, and that she would hold the other party responsible for what they had done. I just assumed Tina was talking about the driver who had caused the accident. But if she thinks hurting someone close to you gets your attention . . . it's twisted, but it might make sense to her."

"Madison said her brakes gave out before she lost control of the car."

Michael grasped Alex's arm. "Come with me."

Alex pulled away and said, "Give me a minute. I want to tell Madison we're leaving."

Detective Morgan met Michael and Alex at the front

desk of the police station and escorted them to a small room where they could talk privately. He listened intently as they shared their suspicions about Tina. Michael shared his knowledge of the threatening messages directed at Alex, the fueled comments Tina had made at dinner, and their theory about Madison's accident.

"These are serious accusations against a police officer. What proof do you have?" Detective Morgan asked, sizing up Michael and then focusing his attention on Alex.

"We only have the threatening messages," Michael said. Alex noticed dark circles under his eyes and guessed he looked pretty much like she felt.

"And the card and flowers she sent to the hospital," Alex added.

"You don't know for sure that she sent them." Detective Morgan looked from Michael to Alex. Reluctantly he said, "I'll have a conversation with her, okay?"

Friday

By Friday, Alex was exhausted. She had spent every night over the past week at the hospital to keep tabs on Madison. Detective Morgan had yet to find Tina. Alex skirted the conversation every time Madison brought it up, but she was running out of her reserve of excuses.

"Alex, please tell me what is really going on. Why do you feel it necessary to sleep here every night? The nurses are taking great care of me, I promise. And you look exhausted. You need some real sleep in your own bed."

Alex pulled her chair alongside the bed and reached for Madison's hand. "Do you remember when we talked about the fact that sometimes my research elicits threatening responses?"

"Sure."

"And do you remember asking me if any of it freaked me out?"

"I do, yes."

Alex paused, trying to find the right words. "I think I'm freaking out now."

"Why?"

"Because I don't think your accident was an accident."

"What? What do you mean?"

"I think Tina may be holding a vendetta against me about her late partner, Anne, and that she meddled with your brakes to try to hurt you." Madison listened intently as Alex filled in the gaps for her.

"Ok, *I'm* officially freaked out. What do we do now?" Madison asked.

"Nothing we really can do. Detective Morgan told me he would contact me when he knew something more."

Madison leaned forward to cup Alex's face and give her a tender kiss. "Thank you for staying here with me, watching over me." The warmth from Madison's gaze and fingers made Alex's heart expand. The feeling of being connected to her spread to the ends of her fingers and toes. Madison raised the blanket, inviting Alex to join her. Mindful of the monitoring cables and cords, Alex carefully crawled into the bed and settled herself against Madison's side. With her head resting on Madison's pillow, she quickly fell asleep.

Alex felt something cold and hard pressed against her temple. When she started to move her free hand to her head, she heard a rough, muffled voice.

"Make a sound and you're dead."

Alex's eyes shot open but only found darkness. A small sliver of light shone beneath the closed door. As her mind escaped its slumber, she realized she was still in bed with Madison. She froze.

Without moving her head, she shifted her gaze to Madison's face and found her eyes wide open and her mouth gagged. A tear formed at the corner of her eye, but her body didn't move, except for her ragged breathing. Alex rested on her side with her right arm invisible under the blankets. She slid her fingers around Madison's wrist and squeezed. Madison closed her eyes and tears slid down her cheek. Alex needed to protect Madison. She pushed her fear away and concentrated on the figure standing over her.

"Tina?" Alex whispered. The pressure against her head increased.

"What?" Tina spat the word.

Confirmation received. Callie and Michael had been right. Tina wanted to hurt her and Madison for Anne's sake. And there was no one here to help them. Alex's mind went into overdrive conjuring up multiple scenarios of how this night might play out. She had to do something.

"What do you want?" Alex asked cautiously.

"I want you to pay. I've heard the news. All this praise for how smart you are makes me sick. Where was all this mind power two years ago when we really needed it? Huh?" Her voice faltered.

So many logical reasons, scientific and operational, flashed through Alex's mind, but she knew none of them would help Tina right now. She had to find a way to connect with her on some deeper level. Michael's words came back to her.

"You don't have to do this, Tina. This can't be who you really are. You're a cop. You vowed to protect and serve people and keep them safe. Michael says you are one of the good guys and besides, Callie likes you and that in itself speaks volumes. She feels something for you. Somehow you got to her."

Tina said nothing.

Alex dug deeper. "I know losing someone you love hurts like hell."

That hit a button. "You have no idea what this feels like. How could you know? Your life is perfect. You have everything," Tina said.

"My life is far from perfect, Tina. My dad died when I was in high school, and I was lost for a long time." Tina released the gun from Alex's forehead but kept it pointed at her. Alex shifted slightly to face her. With that sliver of light from under the door, Alex could make out Tina's face. Her eyes were dark and glassy. Her gaze was intense.

"What do you mean, you were lost?" she asked.

She's caught, hook, line, and sinker. Now, how do I keep her here? Alex rapidly deliberated on what to say. Her gut tightened, and she swallowed hard. Alex unlocked and opened a door in her mind that she vowed never to open again.

"Counselors couldn't help me cope, and my mom was afraid I was going to hurt myself, so she made the decision to have me committed. I was hospitalized for six months." She heard a sound escape Tina. It sounded like a whimper. She saw Tina wipe at her eyes and lower the gun ever so slightly.

"You made it through this hell?" Tina's voice cracked as she started crying.

"It wasn't easy. There was a long time when I wanted to die, to be with him again, but I did make it through, yes. And you can too, Tina. I know you can. I bet it's what Anne would want for you, just like my dad wanted for me."

As her lover's name escaped Alex's lips, Tina broke down. "I miss her so much." She slumped to the floor and started sobbing. Her gun slipped from her hand.

Before Alex could make a move for the gun, men rushed into the room. They pushed Tina the rest of the way to the floor until she was lying flat. Someone flipped on the room's overhead light, and Alex was momentarily blinded. A nurse was talking to Madison while she moved her hands all over her, inspecting her. She had already removed the gag.

Alex saw that the two men were police officers. They escorted Tina out of the room. Alex realized she was still clutching Madison's wrist. When Madison turned to face her, tears flooded Alex's face. She and Madison cried together.

When they had regained their composure, they remained side by side. Words were neither adequate nor necessary. Alex made a renewed vow to herself to never let go of this woman. She now knew for certain she loved Madison, wholly and completely.

Chapter
Fifteen

Saturday

In the early hours of Saturday morning the sky began to lighten and bring more natural light into the room. Detective Morgan was kind enough to give Alex and Madison some time to regroup after the incident before taking their statements. He also conceded to Alex when she refused to leave Madison's side as Madison provided her account of what had happened. Alex learned that while she was talking to Tina, Madison had pressed her call button. Cara, the nurse with the kind face, had come to check on her but when she found the closed door, seemingly blocked, she had returned to the nursing station to turn on the room's camera.

When the camera came online, Cara saw a figure leaning over the bed and immediately invoked the security protocol. The police had arrived on the floor within minutes. Watching and listening, they timed their entrance into the room at the precise moment Tina had dropped her gun.

After the police had left, Cara checked on Madison. Finding everything to her satisfaction, Cara left the room without another word, pulling the door closed behind her. Alex and Madison sat in the stillness for a long moment before Madison broke the silence.

"I'm so sorry, Alex." The empathy in Madison's expression told Alex she was talking about more than what had happened over the last few hours. "Are you really okay?"

"Yes, I am." Alex gave Madison a reassuring smile. "It was the help I needed at the time. I don't think about it anymore. I'm not even sure why it came out when it did. It just felt right, you know?"

"I think it came out at exactly the right time."

They talked more about the events of the previous night but as late morning rolled around, Madison urged Alex to go home and rest. The darkening circles around Alex's eyes emphasized her tiredness. Alex resisted until Madison rang her call button. Cara came running and when Madison gave her the eye, she jumped in to gang up on Alex, citing some excuse about her patient needing rest and about abusing the rules around visiting hours.

Alex glared at the nurse before looking back at Madison and said, "You both suck. You know that, right?"

Madison laughed and pointed to the door, "Go."

"You," pointing a finger at Cara, "I used to like. And

you," pointing a finger at Madison, "So *boss-y*," said Alex, exaggerating the word as she headed out the door.

Wednesday

Alex was thankful for an uneventful start to the week. She returned to checking in on Madison during the approved visiting hours, making a point to seek out Cara on every visit to thank her for taking such good care of Madison.

Alex was seated at her desk reviewing Patricia's morning reports when Trevor walked in.

"Detective Morgan called and asked to see you and Michael today at the station if possible."

"Do I have time?" asked Alex.

"I made time for you at eleven o'clock."

"And Michael?"

"Already confirmed."

Alex smiled, "What would I do without you?"

"You would be lost without me," said Trevor as he swooped back out of the room.

Alex looked at her reports, and Trevor's words echoed in her mind. *Lost.* A warm sensation of appreciation started in her chest and spread through her body. She took a moment to look outside. *How did I not see this before? I can do this. I can have it all. Work will be demanding, nothing new there, but I can make more time for the people who mean something to me. I can do this.* Her smile spread as she refocused on her work.

Alex and Michael arrived at the police station just before the top of the hour. They were escorted by a young police officer into a small private room. Detective Morgan arrived minutes later and took a seat across the table from them.

"Thanks for coming in," he said and acknowledged both of them with a nod. "Over the past four days since taking Tina into custody, we have searched her apartment, car, and station locker, and we've spoken with her colleagues and neighbors. We have statements from both of you and from Madison and Callie. We spoke at length with Tina's psychiatrist, who reluctantly divulged that you and Callie had been a regular topic of discussion in Tina's sessions, Alex. Madison's name came up only recently.

"The doctor shared that, in her sessions, Tina never directly threatened to harm anyone, but the doctor agreed that it was plausible for Tina to believe she could help Anne in some way by holding you, Alex, accountable or perhaps that by causing you pain by hurting Madison, it would help her cope. Her compromised mental state could have prompted her to put her thoughts into action."

Detective Morgan said, "When I interrogated Tina and crafted a story of motive for her, she had very little to say. She sat quietly, staring into space, almost as if she was relieved it was all over. She signed a confession without any hesitation.

"The suspect we had been following associated with the IP address and the threatening emails was one of Tina's confidential informants. It wasn't difficult to get him to point the finger at Tina when the district attorney offered him a deal."

Michael and Alex sat in silence until Detective Morgan stopped talking and closed the manila folder in front of him.

"What will happen to her?" asked Alex.

"I've spoken to the DA. He wants to position a case for impaired mental capacity and with her doctor's testimony of clinical depression, seek psychiatric care for Tina. Best-case scenario."

Alex was at a loss for words other than to thank Detective Morgan for his help. She walked out of the room silently at Michael's side.

Sitting with Alex in the car before leaving the police station, Michael stared straight ahead and said, "I knew she was struggling. I should have paid more attention to her. I thought she was embellishing stories, so I ignored half the stuff she told me. Had I actually listened to her, I might have seen the signs. It was my job to watch out for anything or anyone that might put you or your research at risk. It was my job to protect you from this sort of thing, and I have failed miserably. I'm so sorry, Alex."

"This isn't your fault, Michael. No one could have foreseen how this would play out. Tina manipulated you, just like she manipulated everyone around her." Alex thought of Callie. As Michael drove them back to work, Alex called Callie and asked her to come to the hospital that afternoon.

Alex was sitting on the edge of the hospital bed, holding Madison's hand, when Callie arrived. Callie hugged her tightly and took a seat by the window. She listened intently as Alex relayed the information Detective Morgan shared with her earlier.

After Alex was finished, Callie said, "Tina was behind this the whole time?" She looked at Alex in both disbelief and incredible sadness. Regardless, Alex felt responsible for it, and her best friend's response stabbed at her.

"I am sorry. It was because of me that both of you were hurt," Alex said.

Callie looked defeated but shrugged it off in true Callie fashion. "I'm just glad we're all still here to talk about it."

Madison squeezed Alex's hand and said, "We're okay." Alex felt her saying so much more.

Thursday

By the following week, Madison was well enough to be discharged. Alex and Heather were in the room when Cara brought Madison the last of the paperwork to sign. Madison reached for her crutches, and Alex noticed how difficult it was for her to manage due to her sore ribs.

"Why don't you come stay with me until you're better able to use those things? I can get you anything you need."

"That's a good idea, Madison. You may need some help in the beginning," Heather chimed in.

"Are you sure, Alex?" Madison searched Alex's face for any indication to the contrary.

"I'm absolutely sure."

Alex ducked out of the room to thank Cara one last time before leaving. By the time she got back to the room, Madison was being helped into a wheelchair by a young male nurse.

"Seriously, I can walk out of here," Madison argued.

"It is hospital policy, ma'am," the young man answered.

"Ma'am? How old do you think I am?" Madison's voice squeaked. Her reaction made Alex laugh out loud.

Madison shot her a glare. "This isn't funny." Alex pursed her lips trying to muffle the next laugh that threatened to erupt.

"I got this," Alex motioned toward the young man. "Giving him a hard time, I see. He's just doing his job," Alex teased.

"I was just trying to save him some time so he could go do his job somewhere else. Can you believe he called me ma'am? What's with that? How old do you have to be to be called ma'am? Seriously?"

Alex placated Madison the entire length of the hallway.

When they arrived at Alex's house, Alex wasted no time in preparing the living room for the essentials Madison would need to avoid going up and down the stairs. She pulled out the sofa bed, fitted it with sheets, a comforter, extra blankets, and plush pillows. She rearranged the furniture to allow for easy access to and from the make-shift bed to the hallway and to the bathroom. She didn't want Madison to worry about bumping into anything while she learned to navigate her way around with her new crutches.

Madison took two weeks off work to allow her ribs to heal enough to be able to use the crutches on her own. Alex asked Trevor to keep her updated, and she set up video calls with Patricia for their team updates. Alex and Madison began settling into a new routine, together. Alex slept on the loveseat because she was worried any movement on her part would cause discomfort for Madison. Madison convinced her after only two nights of pleading that she wanted Alex to sleep beside her. Alex finally gave in.

Alex was the first one up every morning. She quietly navigated her way to the kitchen to start the coffee and feed Moose and Kenzie. She took the dogs with her to the barn to feed the horses. When she came in from the barn, she helped Madison get ready for the day and then prepared breakfast for both of them.

Alex found she enjoyed working from home and found herself quite productive while Madison rested. When it was lunchtime, Alex fixed lunch and brought their plates to the table while Madison made her way from the living room.

"What is it?" Alex asked when she saw a look of frustration on Madison's face.

"Aren't you getting tired of being my maid, cook, and bottle washer?" Madison asked.

"Where did that come from?" Alex asked.

Madison threw an arm in the air. "I'm totally encroaching on every aspect of your life by being here. Your living room is in shambles, you've had to adjust your whole routine, your dogs, your horses, and don't even get me started on work. How are you possibly staying up to speed with everything in the lab by working remote?"

Alex reached for Madison's hand. "Hey, I'm doing just fine here. We both know the makeshift living room is temporary, and I'm getting plenty of work done in the morning and afternoon when you're napping." Alex squeezed her hand. "And, truth be told, I'm getting in extra rides during the afternoons between check-in calls with Trevor and Patricia. I've never been able to ride during the week before." Alex put a finger to her lips. "Shh, don't tell anybody."

Madison tried to disguise a smile. Her shoulders relaxed and she sank back in her chair. "Are you sure you are okay with all of this? I feel like I've overstayed my welcome."

"Am I making you feel that way?" Alex asked, sounding concerned.

"God no. That's the point. You've been nothing short of amazing. I'm just afraid you'll wake up one morning and decide you've had enough."

Alex grinned as a thought occurred to her.

"What?" Madison asked.

"It's my turn," Alex said.

"What do you mean?"

"It's my turn to help you, so let me."

Madison sighed.

"It's not so easy to accept help, is it?"

Madison shook her head.

"I'm glad that's settled. Now, finish your lunch and get ready for your nap so I can go riding."

"You're actually enjoying this, aren't you?" Madison asked.

"You bet I am."

Alex's phone chirped and she looked at the screen. "Oh my god."

"Is everything ok?" Madison asked.

Alex looked up with an incredulous expression on her face. "The Phase 1 prelim was just released."

"And?" Madison asked.

"And the trial is producing fantastic results, even beyond my initial projections," Alex said. "We are so close to a breakthrough, Madison. I can feel it." Alex jumped up. "I need to get David and Michael on the phone." Halfway out of the room she looked back at Madison. "You'll be ok?"

"Go." Madison used her hand to motion her out of the room.

Alex returned with a pleased look on her face. She walked straight to Madison, placed her hands on her cheeks and gave her a kiss. She wandered around the room as she shared her conversation. "The FDA gave us approval to fast track the trials to Phase 2. We'll be moving ahead with the in-vitro studies without delay. David gave the green light to start recruiting more patients and, wait for it, he told me he was proud of me. Can you believe that?"

"Well, it's about time."

"I know we won't have final confirmation until we know it's safe and effective within a larger population of human subjects. But just the thought that we may have a potential cure in our hands . . ." Alex's voice cracked. She stopped moving and her eyes filled with tears.

Madison motioned for Alex to sit next to her.

"I am so happy you're here right now. There's no one else I'd rather be with to celebrate this news," Alex said.

"Hearing that makes me so happy, Alex. And when I get out of these bandages," her eyes swept over Alex's body, "I promise to help you celebrate properly."

"Oh yeah?" Alex's eyes widened.

"You can count on it. Now get in here and snuggle with me." Alex climbed into bed and wrapped Madison in her arms.

"Did Michael have any concerns?" Madison asked.

Alex immediately wanted to set her mind at ease. "Nothing to worry about there."

"Good."

Everything was finally falling into place. In that moment Alex was overcome with emotion and felt she would bust at the seams with a secret she could no longer contain. "I love you, Madison."

Madison tensed and for a second Alex was afraid she had done something wrong, "Is it okay that I said that?"

"It's more than okay. Can I just hold on to that for right now?"

It didn't take long before Madison's breathing slowed, and she fell asleep. Alex hugged Madison tighter and she felt her body warm from the inside out.

Friday

With another workweek finished, Alex opened the Chinese takeout containers she had brought home with her and divvied up the food onto two plates. Finishing week eight of her recovery, Madison was back to work part time and getting around much better on her own. She had become a pro with the crutches and needed little help from Alex to navigate through the house. At her checkup earlier in the day, her doctor had commented on how impressed she was by how well Madison was recovering. The doctor replaced her hard cast with a soft one and gave her a boot to wear. Alex noticed it right away.

"Sexy boot you have there," Alex said, as she looked Madison up and down. "Doesn't hold a candle to your suit and heels though."

"You miss my heels?" Madison asked with a playful grin.

"I miss *everything* about your heels," Alex added, her voice dropping to a growl. "I miss how you look in heels, and I miss how it makes me feel when I look at you in heels." Alex had been dodging any sexual thoughts about Madison because she knew Madison needed time to recover from her accident, but over the last week it had been getting harder and harder to curb her need to feel Madison against her and to touch her in that way. She shook her head as if hoping the sheer motion would expel the thoughts from her mind. Madison smiled at her with a look of understanding as if she read her thoughts loud and clear.

"Let's eat," said Alex.

Over a bite of Crab Rangoon, Madison asked, "How was your day?"

"Detective Morgan called me today. Tina's sentencing date has been set. The district attorney has all the evidence he needs to charge Tina for the threatening messages, tampering with your car, and the incident at the hospital. He's confident it will settle out of court, and she will serve her time in a hospital where she will get the help she needs."

"It's still hard for me to wrap my mind around what happened. It's so sad." Madison reached across the table to squeeze Alex's hand.

Feeling a kinship with Tina, Alex added, "I hope Tina finds her way."

"It sounds like there's a lot of people willing to help her do just that. Oh, before I forget. You need to call your sister. She told me to tell you that it is way past time for a visit."

"She's giving you messages for me now?" Alex raised her eyebrow and laughed.

"Maybe. You just need to learn to deal with it," Madison said and laughed back. "What's the latest on your clinical trials?"

"They are going really well. The statistical analysis of the results supports the stated conclusion. We recorded a 90-95% success rate so far in the Phase 1 group. As you well know, we will need to monitor the Phase 2 patients for at least a year before we can officially publish any results. When we get to about six months, however, we should have enough data to confidently take our sample size and extrapolate what the success rate will be for the rest of the patient population."

Madison clinked her glass with Alex's.

"What?" Alex asked, as she tried to discern the look on Madison's face.

"I love your sexy brain."

"What?" Alex asked, as she snickered.

Madison's expression turned serious, "What I mean is, I love you, Alex."

Alex let her words sink in. She looked at Madison and said, "I love you too. I'm utterly and completely gone." Finally, the words rolled off her tongue without effort.

In between the next couple of bites, Alex said, "So, this is what it's like to come home, sit down, eat dinner together, and talk about our day, huh?"

"This is it," Madison confirmed. "Is this enough for you?"

Alex set her fork beside her plate and rested her chin on her folded hands. She gave Madison a pensive look.

"Do you remember the conversation we had the first day you brought in lunch for us to my office?" asked Alex.

"I do," said Madison, apprehensively.

"You used an analogy about reading a book and skipping over the middle and going right to the end to see how the story ends." Alex watched Madison.

"I remember."

"I understand now, and it's because of you. You've given me so much more than I ever imagined possible. You make me want to live in the here and now. Experiencing 'this' with you, without feeling the need to plan out what's next or even be compelled to know the ending, is a luxury I have not been accustomed to. No matter how our story ends, 'this', right here right now, is worth it," Alex maintained eye contact with Madison, "but no, it isn't enough for me."

Madison's expression quickly changed to one of desperate confusion.

Alex quickly added, "Enough for me is knowing that you have everything you want." Freeing herself from any lingering ties to the past, Alex said, "I want to give you everything you want, Madison."

"*Everything?*" Madison swallowed hard.

"Yes, everything. I want to give you the family that you want."

Tears formed in Madison's eyes as she whispered, "Are you absolutely sure, Alex?"

Alex slid her chair closer and her hands came to rest on Madison's knees. "Yes. I've always thought I needed a plan for things to work out and yet from the moment you walked into my world, I've had absolutely no clue what I'm doing, and it couldn't have been more perfect. You couldn't be more perfect. Sweetheart, you mean the world to me, and I am in love with all of you, Madison Thornton. I am so lucky you didn't give up on me."

Madison wiped her eyes. "Do you want to get lucky again?" she asked mischievously.

"Do you feel up to it?" Alex felt a repressed twinge spark low in her belly.

"Oh yeah." With a twinkle in her eyes, Madison shot her that seductive look that made Alex's insides do a familiar somersault. She anticipated and welcomed her body's response to her lover's secret promise.

"I am *so* lucky," Alex repeated with a big grin on her face.

"You are so *loved*."

Epilogue

Five Years Later

Saturday

Alex woke early and walked into the kitchen to make coffee and feed the dogs. Hot mug in hand and dogs in tow, she made her way to the barn to tend to the horses. She stood in the aisleway listening to the sounds of early morning, including that of the horses eating their grain. She walked to the doorway and leaned against its frame and took a deep breath. She inhaled the sweet smell of hay, grass, and dew. Her thoughts drifted to her dad.

"It's been a long time since we've talked, Dad. I met someone to share my life with. Mom and Amber like her. She's smart and funny, and she fills me with joy in so many ways. She challenges me, in a good way, in a way that makes me better." Alex paused. "My heart shattered into a thousand pieces when you died. I didn't realize how broken I was until Maddie came along. Maddie helped me see a different version of myself, one who could unlock those dark places and break through the pain and fear I've held onto for so long. She made me feel safe enough to let down my walls. I don't know why she took a chance on me, but I'm so glad she did. I feel the love she has for me. She loves me like you did, Dad. She makes me feel whole again, and I'm moving forward."

Alex smiled. "And, Dad, we did it. We found a way to beat breast cancer. The news is calling it the medical breakthrough of the century." Alex shook her head. "I don't know about that, but I do know that it's helping a lot of people. Most importantly, I've had a breakthrough, Dad. I'm finding the good parts of me again. I'm ashamed to admit I kept a lot of myself hidden for a long time from the people who care about me. And I've hurt people, Dad. I spent so much time shutting my feelings off to survive after losing you, I almost forgot what it was like to love someone and to have them love me in return. It became second nature to push relationships away, justifying it by using my research as an excuse. But those same people believed in me even when I didn't believe in myself."

Alex wiped her eyes. "I'm aware now that I don't have to go it alone for fear of letting people in and getting hurt. Had I never opened myself up to new possibilities, I would have missed out on so much. I believe I've become a better person because of it, and I hope that makes you proud." Alex gazed up at the sky. "I miss you."

A horse whinnied and Alex went back into the barn. All four horses looked as if they were standing witness to her private conversation. Dunkin nodded and Alex walked over to him to stroke his head. He stilled a moment and stared at her with a big, beautiful brown eye.

"We are going to be just fine," Alex said. She kissed him on the cheek and left the barn to go back to the house.

Madison walked into the kitchen, dressed and ready to ride. She commented on how good the coffee smelled. She folded her arms around Alex and gave her a kiss. Alex's senses commanded attention as the softness of Madison's body pressed against her and her hands caressed her back. Alex took a moment to breathe in the sweet smell of her perfume, then handed Madison a cup of coffee and leaned against the counter.

"Have I told you lately how sexy you look in that outfit?" Alex let her eyes slowly roam over Madison from head to toe.

"Maybe once or twice." Madison's grin sprouted into a smile.

"M'm m'm." Alex shook her head and looked Madison up and down again.

"Keep looking at me like that and we'll never get out of here," Madison teased. Alex laughed and pushed herself from the counter.

"Come on, girls!" Alex yelled into the next room. "It's time for your lesson."

Twin girls came running into the kitchen. "We're ready, Moms," the girls said in stereo.

Alex said, "Let's go then."

"Can we still go play with Aunt Callie's puppies after our lesson?" Ashley asked.

"And take Moose and Kenzie too?" Brooke chimed in.

"Well, we can't break with tradition, now can we?" Alex puckered her lips and crossed her eyes, making the girls giggle.

Madison smiled contently and followed close behind as Alex, Kenzie, and Moose chased the girls to the barn.

ABOUT THE AUTHOR

Photo © Dawn MacGibbon 2020

Terri Cutshall was born and raised in Pennsylvania, where she earned a degree in Pharmacy. She's worked as a pharmacist in clinical and commercial operations for most of her career. When not working or writing, she enjoys her family and spending time with her animals or traveling internationally. She currently lives near Raleigh, North Carolina, with her wife, her horse, and two dogs.

Follow me on Twitter:
@terricutshall

Follow me on Facebook:
https://www.facebook.com/authorterricutshall

Email me:
tcutshallauthor@gmail.com

Instagram:
@cutshallterri

Also by TERRI CUTSHALL

Made in the USA
Middletown, DE
21 January 2025

69378251R00135